Birth

Birth

Once, Upon A New Time Book One

Donna Russo Morin

Other works by Donna Russo Morin

Birth (Once, Upon A New Time Book One)
The Courtier of Versailles
Gilded Summers
The Flames of Florence (Da Vinci's Disciples Book Three)
The Competition (Da Vinci's Disciples Book Two)
Portrait of a Conspiracy (Da Vinci's Disciples Book One)
The King's Agent
To Serve a King
The Secret of the Glass

To all who see magic…
and believe it.

Contents

Chapter I

DRIVEN

The curved, sharp tip of the falchion blade sliced him from elbow to shoulder; in the strange, slowness of time on a battlefield, he watched blood pump from his limb with every beat of his heart.

He knew pain, the yell of it stung the back of his throat; he ignored both. He stumbled, tripped over bodies and parts, hearts no longer pumping. His broadsword sliced through any Elf daring to stand before him, dying a little each time his blade... his hand... cut off their life.

He could no longer guard himself; his shield plummeted from the damaged arm, rendered nearly useless by the blade's hard slice. His anger rose up, equally as hard, equally as impenetrable. His swung his blade before him, all the defense he had, a harsh swish that cut the air and all else that stood in his path.

The cry beckoned him ever onward. His own moaning filled his ears, like those of so many others on the field. Sword clanged against sword, or ax, or shield. The dying screamed for their mothers or the mercy of their gods. Yet the plea found him again and again. High-pitched, somehow subdued; in the lament, he heard pain unbearable, courage unshakeable. He would find that voice. Count Witon é Lahkrok would find who made such a sound... and save them.

His long legs made short shrift of the blood-soaked ground as he stepped around opponents locked in near mindless battle, moving ever closer to the front lines. The cataclysm thickened; he banged and ricocheted against bodies—a horde packed and locked in combat—his footsteps squelching in bloodied mud.

Witon lost his way, a red veil of blood muddling in silver-grey eyes. Confused by the mass of bodies—Human and Elf—fighting in pairs and bunches unrecognizable from one to the other. The beauty of his land lay in desolation, camouflaged by the conflagration of bodies. Pain burst in his gullet, a sledgehammer blow from within. How hard he had tried to stop this war; how miserably he had failed... a failure reeking of excrement and withering life.

"Would someone help me... please?"

It came again. That voice, a man's, but not quite. A boy?

"Please?"

Witon's head spun; droplets of blood and sweat sputtered out from his skin, from tangled strands of long hair.

A hand taller than most men, at least two above most Elves, his view of the vista lay unobstructed. His gaze searched as the pleading reverberated. So close now; he knew it, felt it.

"Where are ye?" Witon called out, a boom above the din. "I will help, I swear it."

Truth rang clear in his words, the longing for the killing to stop.

"H... here."

It came as little more than a squeak now, yet the desperation in it grew ever louder.

It was enough.

Witon whirled to his left, sidling now as his head volleyed left and right, avoiding a swinging sword, an avalanching ax. His foot struck and held; upon stone or body, it made no difference. He faltered, bending at the waist to balance, arms pinwheeling.

He saw him then.

In a pool of blood-like fluid, greenish and thick, with flecks of red, the creature lay. One inert arm lolled on the ground, nearly cut clean off... bone hacked in two, muscle ends withering. Just a thin layer of flesh joined limb to body; a thin layer of light green flesh.

Witon, struggling for breath after the difficulties of the search, stared down, unable to move, for he knew not what manner of being he had found.

Pale green eyes, swollen with tears and red-rimmed, beseeched him, pain writ harshly upon the strange face. Roused by the imploring gaze, Witon stirred; it mattered not at all what it was, only that it needed his help. It was the way of him, the way he had pledged to live.

"I am here." Witon squatted, leather creaking, armor rattling. Throwing his sword from his hand, he scooped his long, thick arm beneath the injured being and lifted him up as he would thin twigs of kindling, throwing the creature over his uninjured shoulder. "I will get you help."

Rising up, hitching the injured body higher up, secured by its own weight, Witon turned from the front lines of the battle.

In the world of Minra Erna, the air forever crackled with all forms of magic; but few had ever seen the sort Witon wrought in that moment.

He walked.

He walked with grey eyes narrowed, glowing silver. He walked with thick lips clenched in a thin, bloodless line, jaw muscles jumping. He walked with huge, long strides that proclaimed he would permit no obstruction. No one dared try.

They parted for him. Elves and Humans alike lowered their weapons, mouths dropping to gaping dark maws against pale faces blotched with blood and dirt, astonishment blighting the antagonism they shared.

"Belamay!" Witon cried the name, trudging through the forest of decimation. "Belamay! I need you, Belamay!"

Silence answered; the battlefield hushed, became a place of worship. In the wake of screams and clangs, Witon's voice rang out.

"Belamay, please!"

"Here! I am here, Witon!"

From the back of the field, the fully armored warrior stepped out of the crowd, near the edge of the meadow where once green grass—now torn earth, black with green and red blood—met thick and lush forest. Dark eyes peered out the visor slit; a long shaft of midnight black hair fell out the back, hanging to the soldier's knees.

"What in the name of the Great Stars...?"

"Do not ask." Witon stepped towards Belamay, nothing but the small, battered body between them. "He... she... it..."

Witon shook his head; a grind of his teeth, a clench of his bruised eyelids.

He opened them; with naught but clear sight, he stabbed Belamay with his piercing gaze.

"*We* need you."

The soldier's dark eyes flicked between Witon and the creature in his arms, but only for a moment.

"This way."

Witon followed, breath hitching with relief.

"Fosrin!" Witon shrieked the name of his sergeant, head once more whirling this way, that way.

Within seconds, the brawny young man stood stiffly by Witon's side.

"Sir." A bark of obedience, a bow of his helmeted head.

Witon leaned close, voice low. "Get our men out of... *this*. I see no good end for us, for either side. But do it gradually, a few at a time, no more."

The sergeant raised his head and lifted his visor. He need not remove his helmet for Witon to see the dissatisfaction written on his ruddy face. It glinted there in the narrowed, darkening gaze, all too transparent.

"Just do it," Witon hissed, turning without another word, following Belamay once more.

Into the trees they ran, dread travelling beside them. Would the creature die before they could give help? Would either Human soldiers or Elven—or worse, both—follow and attempt to stop them? He feared both.

Belamay led them along a thin, rutted pathway. Sunshine dappled the light brown dirt beneath their feet with specks of incongruent brilliance. Then off the path, into a clearing, but not an empty one.

Within the copse, horses grazed, reins loosely tied to surrounding trees.

"Give h… let me take the burden while ye mount." Belamay held out hands covered to the elbow with thick brown leather gauntlets, blood-stained and cracking.

As if handling a child, Witon conveyed the creature into Belamay's hands. "Which horse?"

Belamay shrugged. "What does it matter? None of them are mine."

"Hah!" Witon barked a laugh, a blessed moment of humor in a world devoid of it.

He reached for the saddle horn on the largest black destrier, knowing it must bear the weight of two, and hefted himself up with one graceful motion.

"To me," he said, settled in the seat, leaning down with arms held out in a cradle.

Belamay delivered the creature back to his savior, untied the reins of their horse, and handed those up as well.

"With me!" Twirling onto a bay shire, snapping the leather tongs, Belamay led them away in a flurry.

Witon blinked, a slowly closing of lids in relief, words of gratitude to the Great Stars spoken in his mind. But their exit did not come soon enough.

As if it gave chase, the sounds of the battle—the resumption he feared most—rose up behind them and his heart suffered yet another wound. With a slap of the reins, he rushed from it.

Chapter II

URGENCY

The small manor house nestled within a grove of pine, their prickly needles just beginning the slow turn to autumn auburn glory.

"Talia?" Belamay bellowed, the call rising above the thunder of the horses charging forward through the small dirt courtyard. The soldier pulled hard on the reins at the front arched door, jumping from the bay even before it had come to a stop.

Grunting, throwing off the heavy, encompassing helmet, flushed pale skin revealed, Belamay yelled once more, impatience mingling with insistence. "Talia!"

The door burst open and the young, aproned maid stood in its threshold. Blue eyes round, bulging, held reflections of her mistress covered in blood, of Witon with a bloodier creature flopping in his lap.

Belamay could see the shock writ so plainly on the young girl. For nearly two years, Talia had served in Belamay's home, never knowing Belamay as the secret soldier she was, the only daughter of a deceased, distinguished warrior, a nobleman and his wife, both lost in a fire years ago. Reaching out, Belamay took Talia's hand gently, giving it a shake.

"Look at me, Talia." She took the girl's other hand, giving both a shake as the maid's loose arms quivered. Dropping her voice, imitating her father with a concoction of command and care, Belamay spoke the girl's name once more: "Talia." It was all she needed.

The pale, bulging eyes turned to her; in them, Belamay gratefully found recognition, cognition.

Belamay dipped her head, eye to eye. "I need you to make for the Dwarf village. 'Tis but a short distance away, but you must run. You must hurry."

The willowy girl's jaw dropped, her head shaking slightly. "The D-Dwarf Village?" With each syllable, Talia's voice squeaked higher.

Belamay nodded slowly, patiently. "Yes. But have no fear. Speak my name to any who would question or cross you, and I swear," here, Belamay took both of Talia's hands and clasped them in hers, as if they prayed as one, "I swear to you, ye will come to no harm."

Talia snapped shut her trembling mouth. She nodded unenthusiastically, not looking wholly convinced.

"That's my girl." Belamay awarded her with a smile. "Ask for Pagmav, he is their healer. Tell him a life needs his hands."

"P... Pagmav?" Talia stuttered on the unfamiliar name, moving slowly, a specter in a dream... a nightmare.

Belamay nodded. "Pagmav, yes." Raising her voice, a clip of harshness crept its way in. She spun the girl by the shoulders, turned her toward the eastward path leading away from the manor, and gave her a soft push. "Go!"

She gave a command, one not to be denied.

Lifting her plain muslin skirt, Talia scampered away without looking back, a child running from the marauding monster of her dreams, or perhaps towards one.

Belamay huffed relief, spinning round.

"Help me, Belamay."

Witon perched—trapped—half-way upon his steed, trying to hold the small, battered body in one hand while he attempted to lower himself from the stately beast with the other, the arm so fiercely injured. The added weight threw off his balance and his body jammed, stuck between on and off.

Belamay ran to him, reaching up and bracing Witon's back with both hands. She planted her boot-clad feet in the packed dirt of the courtyard. With her support, Witon made the descent, the body in his arms now completely limp, but not lifeless. The rapid heartbeat pulsed visibly in the slim neck.

"We cannot wait." Witon ran for the still open door. "We must at least try to stem the bleeding."

Inside the manor, he paused, blinded for a moment after the brilliance of sunlight in the courtyard, then made for the stairs along the west wall, knowing they were there, having climbed them on many an occasion.

He reached the second-floor landing; Belamay's clopping steps followed behind, thudding on the stone like thunderclaps.

"Which room?" he shouted, loudly, urgently.

"The end on the left." Belamay pointed over his shoulder.

Witon rushed ahead, reaching the closed door in seconds, using a large, booted foot to kick it open.

The small, simple room contained a single bed, ready should a guest or passing traveler need accommodation. It held little else save a washstand and a small garderobe.

With a gentleness belying his exigency, Witon placed the creature upon the bed with excruciating tenderness, mindful of the horrifically injured limb.

The tall man hovered over the small creature, looking even smaller upon the large bed, and felt a pull on his heart. "We must save him."

"Him?" Belamay asked from just behind Witon.

Witon brought his broad shoulders up to his ears, nodding. "Yes, I think."

He turned to her, his face smeared with dirt and blood, yet his silver eyes glistened with tears and a furrow ran deep between his downturned brows.

"Some cloths, Belamay, please."

At the washstand, Belamay pulled out every cloth from the shelf below and plunged them into his waiting hands, then turned back, grabbing the terracotta pitcher.

"Be right back," she said over her shoulder, rushing from the room.

Witon stood motionless, cloths clamped in his large hands, looking down, helpless, no notion what to do. But of course, he did. He had been on too many battlefields—seen too many souls die, some in his arms—not to know.

He dropped to his knees by the bed, placing the bunched fabric next to the small body. With a touch as light as a Faerie's, he eased the dangling arm so the ripped ends of flesh abutted each other. The creature stirred; legs thrashing ever so weakly, face crumbling and scrunching with silent pain. Witon turned from it; he could not do what needed to be done if he didn't. There was something in that face... the long, slanted eyes, the small, pointed nose... that begged for his care—and he would give it.

Once the limb was in place, Witon packed it with cloth. Not daring to lift it, he gently covered the wound with wads of material on both sides and on top, material that quickly splotched and stained a strange shade of puce.

With that done—all that he could—Witon lifted a hand, placing it on the creature's forehead; he felt no fever and closed his eyes, feeling another small moment of relief. On opening them again, his face blossomed with surprise, for, even as he stroked the small head, the creature's writhing dissipated. The legs stilled, the face unclenched, as if Witon's touch had worked the magic of some calming elixir. Witon almost smiled... almost.

"Step aside, Sir." A wizened voice reached him from behind. Witon flinched. "If you please."

The speaker stood no taller than Witon's hip, yet something in the very manner of this Dwarf demanded obedience. Witon stepped aside, and the grey-haired, elderly Dwarf took his place. Tucking his long beard into his robe of brown wool, Pagmav—for it could be no other—scanned the injured creature from head to foot.

"'Tis his arm that—" Witon began, or tried to.

Pagmav turned, placing a wrinkled, age-spotted hand upon Witon's arm, looking up with eyes of oak brown. "I know, dear Count, how much you care for this life. Leave it in my hands. I will see to it."

Witon knew nothing of this Dwarf; had never laid eyes on him, yet Pagmav knew him. Witon believed his promise, every word.

"Come, Witon." Belamay took him by the arm as Pagmav's hand released him, pulling gently. "Let him do his work. He will do it well, I swear it to you."

Witon looked down at this wondrous woman, her raven ringlets falling about her round face. In that moment, he felt nothing but gratitude to them both.

"See to your man's wound," the Dwarf healer said without turning round, leaning against the bedside, removing all manner of tools and devices from the large leather bag he had brought with him.

With a nod to Pagmav and a last look at the life he prayed to the Stars to save, Witon quit the room, following Belamay's lead.

Chapter III

REST AND RELIEF

"Would you send a page to the field?"

He sat on the edge of her large, canopied bed. She sat behind him, her legs splayed, one on each side of his body, as she cleansed his wound… as she wrapped and tied it with pristine white linen.

Head tilted to the left, his wounded side, Belamay nodded. "What message do ye wish to send?"

Witon shook his head, grime-filled russet hair swinging against now bare shoulders.

"No message, just…" his chin fell toward his bare chest, "… just an accounting. Of the fighting, if it still continues, of the numbers left on the field, whether or not my men made it safely away."

Belamay finished her ministrations, tying off the cloth, tightly enough to ebb the flow of slow, trickling blood, but not too tightly as to cause discomfort. With a grunt of satisfaction, she shimmied around her lover's body and stood before him, still dressed in her soldier's garb.

Leaning down, she took his wide chin in her hand and lifted it, her large black eyes meeting his pale ones.

"I will do so if you promise to lie down. To rest, at least, if not to sleep."

Witon looked upon the face that brought him such joy, that filled his heart to bursting, and knew it for its softness as well as for the strength behind it.

"To rest at least," he agreed.

Belamay sniffed, with a small shrug of her shoulders. It was the best she could expect from him; she knew it as truth. But she took not one step from him, and he rolled his eyes.

Now it was his turn to shimmy, up and fully onto the bed, laying his pate upon the silk and satin pillows. He gazed at her smugly.

"Fine," Belamay snipped, a mother to a child. "Stay there or I will tell ye naught I learn."

Once more, Witon felt his eyes roll, but this time he found them heavy. Perhaps to close them for a few moments would not be such a bad thing after all.

* * *

"Mayhaps we should let him sleep." A man's voice, thin and with the slightest of warbles.

"No, he would want to know as soon as possible."

That voice he knew; the dulcet tones of his Belamay brought him up from the void.

Witon's eyes fluttered open. They stood right beside him, Belamay and Pagmav, observing him like a specimen in a cage.

"What do I want to know?" he asked, gently easing himself up to a sitting position with the use of his good right arm. He squinted at them through dusk's fading light lilting through the slatted shutters with soft, horizontal rays. Two hours he had surrendered to sleep, perhaps more.

"Your young friend," Pagmav croaked.

Any vestiges of sleep Witon threw off like a rough, coarse blanket.

"Does... h... h...?"

"He, oh yes, most definitely a he," Pagmav said, rubbing his face with a long-fingered hand. Witon could see the fatigue, though the Dwarf tried to wipe it away.

Nodding with satisfaction, as if an itch had been scratched, Witon asked, "Does he live?"

"He does," Belamay said quickly. "And he should regain the use of his arm, most of it, at least."

"And as long as he receives care and plenty of rest, he should live a long life, if his Elfish blood has any say in the matter."

"He is... an Elf?" Witon's voice squeaked like that of an adolescent boy.

"Partly." Pagmav waddled to the large, cushioned chair in the near corner and dropped his round body into it, feet lifting from the ground as he scurried backward to rest his small spine. "And part Human."

"No!" The astonished exclamation resounded from both Witon and Belamay.

In this kingdom of Minra Erna there lived Centaurs and Elves, Trolls and Dwarves, Faeries and Brownies, Goblins and Humans, their co-existence in constant discord. At least as long as history had been written. To think two tender souls had risked so much, all for love, was rare... astonishingly rare.

"'Tis true." Pagmav leaned his head back and closed his eyes, but not his mouth. "It is the only half-breed of the kind I have ever seen. It took me a while to understand his physiology."

"But you did, as I knew only you could," Belamay cooed, stepping to the healer and taking his hand. Witon wondered upon the sight; a Human woman tenderly holding the hand of a Dwarf. It bound them, she and Witon; one of the many bonds strengthening their love ever tighter, ever brighter. "There is a hearty dinner waiting for you whenever ye are ready."

Wrinkled lids crinkled with a smile. "Thank you, my dear. I've just suddenly realized how hungry I am."

Even with Belamay's assistance, it took some effort for the tired Dwarf to heft his form from the chair enveloping him with its cushiony succor. At the door, he turned back.

"I meant what I said, he will recover. But it must be under the most recuperative of surroundings... medical supervision, a clean environment, good food. Without all these, all will not be well."

Witon stood—bandaged, eyes rimmed with smudges of fatigue—with an indisputable air. "I swear it to you, Sir, he will receive all he needs and more. By my honor."

Pagmav nodded slowly, contented. None called the honor of Count Witon into question... not a creature alive, whatever sort of creature they may be.

"May I look in on him?" Witon asked, a step behind the elderly Dwarf's tottering feet.

Holding up a single finger, Pagmav conceded, "Look, no more. Do not wake him. He will do so when his body is ready for him to, no sooner."

Witon followed the Dwarf out; as the healer made for the stairs leading down and to the kitchen, Witon crossed the hall, passing well-dressed and healthy-looking servants, two young men and two young women, carrying a copper tub and buckets of hot water into Belamay's room.

Witon almost turned back at the images flashing in his mind's eye, of her curvaceous body submerged in warm water, lathered and slick with fragrant soap. But he needed to see the young creature first. He needed to see he lived.

Slowly, Witon cracked the spare room door open, a drawn-out creak by little-used hinges announced his arrival. Tiptoeing across the room, he stood by the bedside once more. He smiled at profuse signs of efficiency: the cleaned skin; the perfectly measured stitches just visible through the thin linen binding the monstrous wound; the precisely sized pieces of wood bound to the arm in three places, rendering it immovable. He must remember to ask Pagmav how long the bindings needed to stay in place.

A tinge of color blossomed now on the young creature's face, a deeper shade of green, though not the dense green of a full-blooded Elf. But it was enough to gift Witon a breath of crisp relief.

Leaning down, he placed his large hand once more upon the creature's forehead.

"I know not what binds us, my friend," he whispered, a hint of amusement in his low tone, "but bound we are. I know it. I swear fealty to you. I swear to see ye well once more."

As he gently pushed the pin-straight hair—a dark blonde, Witon thought, seeing it through the layers of mud that sullied it—off the creature's face, he thought he saw the thin lips flicker as if in a smile.

It was enough.

Chapter IV

REJOICE AND RENEWAL

He entered her room, calming jasmine and lavender scents assailing him. Still immersed in the tub, Witon saw only her bare shoulders, her thick abundant hair, wet, and pinned atop her head. Steam wafted from the water and her body, a haze of thin, white vapor as if a magical cloud enveloped her. In his mind, in his heart, it surely did.

Belamay smiled when she saw him. "He is well?"

Witon nodded. "He sleeps... a restful sleep."

"'Tis good," Belamay said, rubbing a soapy cloth on a raised arm. "Are you hungry?"

Witon sniffed, amused. He prowled toward her, his appetite increasing with every step.

"Oh, indeed. I am ravenous." He stood at the very side of the tub now, and now he could see through the water, seeing every curve of her naked body, the thatch of dark hair at the 'v' formed by the joining of her long legs. "But not for food."

His eyes narrowed, glowing, a small smile tickling one corner of his full mouth. The pink bloom on Belamay's cheeks spread, not solely from the warmth of the water.

Witon reached out and took the cloth and the lump of soap from her hands. As Belamay rested her arms upon the rim of the tub, Witon rubbed the sweet-smelling square—a mixture of her favored herbs, oil of olives, and soda powder—till the concoction coated the cloth with a thick, foamy lather. Kneeing beside the tub, he began at her neck.

With slow, luxurious strokes, he swiped the cloth from hairline down, sweeping along her lithe form, down across her collarbone to her buoyant breasts, stopping just at the tips of her large, beige nipples. With each caress, Belamay's breath hitched, gained speed, her full breasts heaving each time. Mesmerized by the sight, Witon's gaze flicked from their bounty to his lover's face. She had closed her eyes and opened her mouth with the pleasure he brought her, and the sight sent his already hardened penis straining against his breeches. He would give her more, so much more.

Now he brought the cloth down her shoulders, lifting her arms to lather them top and bottom. His other hand followed, the slick skin of his palm rubbing each arm, up and down, his sinewy forearm grazing each nipple as it passed up, then down, each nub hardening at the touch.

Belamay moaned and Witon knew she needed more, as did he.

He touched the cloth to that exquisite space between each breast, a hollow where all manner of comfort waited. With a slowness that set them both trembling, he lowered the cloth inch by inch along the curve of her abdomen, toward first one hip and then the other and then, finally, to the thatch of hair between her legs, to the swollen lips waiting impatiently for him there.

Witon tossed away the cloth; he needed—he must—feel her for himself. Still kneeling beside the tub, he brushed back the curls falling around her face as Belamay rocked her body, thrusting her pelvis up in need and hope. With his left, he touched her, explored her. The lips slick with her wetness, the clit so engorged, so in need.

"Witon, please..." Her breath a harsh whisper, and he looked up to find her staring at him, the same lust thumping in his heart writ all over her face. He smiled and reached for her hands. One he set to the laces of his breeches, eliciting a low groan in the back of his throat each time she pulled one loose, each time his hardness felt a brush of her fingers. Her other hand he lathered and placed upon her own breast, guiding her to tease her own nipple with her fingers, to draw circles round it, to pinch and squeeze it gently.

Belamay set herself to the task of her pleasure, spinning her taut nipple tween thumb and forefinger, the hand on his laces trembling and shaking.

Witon continued his exploration with his other hand, stroking her clitoris now, back and forth, knowing precisely where to flick, where to press. Belamay groaned harder as she pushed herself against him.

"Oh, Stars, yes," Witon heard his own impassioned voice.

Belamay released the last of his laces, releasing his long, engorged penis and lathered it with her hand, stroking it with the smoothness till it flinched with need, till it began to dribble with the coming explosion.

He looked down at her, their eyes locked in their pleasure. How it enticed him to watch each other as they brought their bodies to ultimate bliss.

Belamay moved her hand from her breast, reached down and took his from her clit. Without releasing his gaze, she took his hand, grasped his middle finger and plunged it into her. Together they groaned, surrendering completely to the pleasure. She helped him as he pumped it in and out for a moment, then moved her own fingers to her abandoned clitoris. Witon broke their gaze long enough to see their hands upon her beauty. Their moans deepened; love and lust burning together in their once again fixed and locked stare.

The small smile reappeared on Witon's lips as he took his right hand and wrapped it around the hand of hers clasping his pulsing member. Together they stroked him. Together they pleasured her. Together they stroked his penis in rhythm with the pumping of his hand inside her, the flicking of her fingers on her clit.

Together they cried out as their fluids of satisfaction spurted forth, wringing every ounce of it, every moment of pleasure, till neither could stand any more.

Witon dropped back on his heels, his head dropping back on his shoulders.

And he began to laugh.

Looking up, he saw her smile, saw her heavy-lidded eyes, both askew and drunk with physical delight and satisfaction.

Witon leaned over the tub and kissed her, languishing in those smiling lips with his own, with his tongue. He kissed her until all the words of love unspoken were spoken in the gesture. He pulled away, laughing again as she slowly opened her eyes, ever more dazed by the love he plied so divinely upon her.

He stood then, though weakly. Depleted, satiated, he kicked off the breeches bunched about his ankles, and climbed in the tub with her, splashing the now tepid water upon the stone floor, the sloshing a lovely accompaniment to her sensual giggles.

She wiggled into the space of his spread legs, as they entwined in each other's arms, heads resting on each other's shoulders as if in surrender.

"Do you ever think we shall make love in any normal way?" she asked against a shoulder that immediately began to shake with laughter.

"By the Stars, I hope not," Witon guffawed.

Together, they finished cleansing each other of the detritus of the battlefield once and for all.

Chapter V

ENOUGH

They barely made it from the tub to the bed, exhausted from a day filled with a lifetime of living. Their bodies ached with the bruises of the battlefield, their spirits too, and yet in their lovemaking, they had found succor. Their exertions brought more fatigue, but of a soothing sort.

Without thought of aught else, they wrapped their naked bodies together among the linens and together they fell, tumbled, into the blissful nowhere of slumber.

"M'lady?" A faint whisper from a timid young female; it did nothing to rouse them, to pull them from the escape of somnolence.

"Ye will have to speak louder than that," the squire tutted, standing just outside the door. With outstretched fingers, he gave the girl a gentle push, tumbling her into the room. Though younger, he had more experience in the widowed Dame Falconick's household; seeing her curled about the manly form of the Count surprised him not at all; he felt only a consequence of envy, toward both.

The willowy blonde flapped a nervous hand at him, but took a few more timid steps into the shadowed room and cleared her throat; the rustling of the floor rushes ceased, her courage faltered.

"M'lady Belamay?" This time, her young, high-pitched voice resonated enough to break the spell.

Head moving slowly at first, hair swishing against the pillow upon which it lay, Belamay stirred, dark eyes blinking open to the grayness of a dawn not yet quite realized. Seeing her young maid before her, Belamay sat up, holding the linen to her naked breasts.

"What brings thee, Clareen?"

Dipping a quick curtsey, Clareen reported her news. "Josem has returned, M'lady. He awaits your presence." She pointed to the door, a gesture—an accusation—as well as an announcement.

"What? What is afoot?" Witon grumbled, rousing, rubbing sleep-swollen eyes as he sat up, not bothering or caring to cover his naked torso, not noticing the appreciative widening of Clareen's eyes as she allowed herself a quick view of the muscled abdomen.

"'Tis Josem." Belamay laid a calming hand upon Witon's arm.

But it did no good. Witon snapped awake, attention bursting upon him.

"Josem," he barked, "bring thee in here, now!"

A command not to be ignored.

A command complied with.

With simple wool cap twisting in his hands, the young boy inched inside, dark hair revealed, a tangled, sweaty mess.

He bowed without grace before the bed, mousey brown eyes remaining cast down.

"What news, Josem, pray tell," Witon asked, more kindly this time, at the sight of the obedient youth. "Does the battle continue?"

"Nay, M'lord." Josem's voice cracked, but from nothing more than puberty. "Dead of night saw its end."

Witon's eyes flicked a sidelong flash at Belamay; she took his hand in hers.

"Who claimed victory, Josem?" The voice that had gone from command to polite request came faintly now... hesitant.

The young page looked up, his bushy brows closing ranks upon his smooth forehead. "No one, M'lord." He shook his head. "Th... there were not enough remaining alive from either camp."

No one spoke. A monster by the name of devastation enveloped the room—an invisible cloud of darkness and blood and evil—and all the air in it.

Witon's vision blurred with tears, but in his mind's eye he saw the meadow littered with bodies, Human or Elf, it mattered not to him. Such desolation was the greatest sin of their times, and it had gone on far too long. The cool tear trickled slowly down his cheek but he gave it no thought, could not even blink his eyes. Wherever his mind took him, there stood all the men who had followed him into that needless battle. Yes, he had given the order for their retreat, yet he could think only of whom he may have lost, for each one was dear to him.

He rose from the bed, impervious to his own nakedness, to Clareen's squeak as she spun round. He placed a hand upon Josem's shoulder and the young boy looked up into the eerie eyes of this lord whom so many, himself included, idolized.

"I must ask yet another mission of you," Witon said, coughing away the catch of emotion in his voice.

With a quick glance at Belamay, Josem gave a quick nod. "I am at your service, M'lord."

"Take my horse and make for my castle."

At this, Josem's eyes bugged from his still boyish face. He looked more fearful now than at any moment he had been in the room.

"Perhaps he could take one of the rounceys in my stable," Belamay suggested, rewarded with a relieved glance from Josem, a fairly inexperienced rider. Belamay kept many such gentler, slower horses on hand for the simple folk of her manor.

Witon waved a hand. "Whatever you would prefer, Josem. But make pace as fast as ye can. Find out who…"

But he could not finish; Witon could not say the words. He dropped back onto the foot of the bed.

"Bring the Count a muster, if you would, Josem." Belamay finished where Witon could not.

Josem gave another of his silent, awkward bows and rushed from the room with Clareen hard on his heels, closing the door in their wake.

Belamay let the linen drop, scurrying on her knees to the end of the large bed, wrapping her entire body about her beloved, one leg on each side of his hips, arms enfolding about his torso, hands clasping tight against his chest.

"You told them to leave. They would have followed your order immediately," she said against his back, where she laid her head.

Witon's breath hitched at her words, at the small glimmer of hope ignited.

"But did the order come soon enough? Did they make haste? Fosrin did not look pleased at the order, perhaps he did not respond quickly enough?" They were not questions he expected her to answer, only ones he could not stop asking himself.

He turned upon the bed, his left hip snuggling into the gulley between her legs. Witon stared at the face he had loved for near to ten full cycles of the moon; the face he longed to see till the end of his days. But would she still want him after he said what he felt? He had to take the chance, he could no longer keep silent.

"I can take this no more," he told her, holding her gaze with his.

Belamay raised a shoulder. "Very well. We shall dress, we shall go ourselv—"

Witon shook his head, long hair thrashing with vehemence. "'Tis not what I mean. I can no longer take what our world has become."

Belamay's face scrunched and she leaned back, as if a few inches of space would gain her some clarity.

"These wars, these animosities between the species, have been a pestilence upon us for far too long." Witon stood then, leaning toward her, hands on the bed, one on each side of her. "It is killing life as we know it. It may kill us all very soon."

Belamay shook her head, dark eyes black saucers in skin turning ever paler. But she spoke not a word in denial. She could not. She knew, as did Witon, about the ever-declining population. The prolific wars were killing the male species, leaving more and more women without mates, without children, bringing them into war themselves, pushed by the need for vengeance, much as Belamay had done. When not at war, pillages, by all breeds, decimated whole villages at a time; the men, the women, and yes, the children. No act had become too barbarous, as no one species could gain control, were allowed control, long enough to stop it.

"I cannot live here anymore." Witon stood tall.

Belamay's ever-widening gaze followed him up. "W... where would you go? There is nowhere in Minra Erna that is not suffering... nowhere that is unsullied by the throes of war."

Witon walked slowly round the side of the bed, feeling the stabbing glare of her eyes upon him. She knew him well enough; he could see the anxiousness, the uncertainty on her face. He crawled onto the bed beside her and took her in his arms.

"I want to leave Minra Erna."

Her gaze pinged back and forth between his eyes and his mouth, as if it were not he behind those strangely silver eyes... as if it was not his mouth that spoke such words.

"Where would you go?" Her question broke the suffocating silence. "There... there is nowhere else. Minra Erna is all. Even the smaller lands are part of it. It was all consumed hundreds of years ago."

Now that she had found her words, she could not seem to stop. She put a hand to his bare chest and pushed against him, pushing against such a notion.

"Will you go into hiding? Is that wh—"

Witon took her mouth with his, his lips caressing hers, his tongue entering and stroking; it was the best way he knew to silence her.

She fought... for half a moment, then capitulated, languished.

When he gently pulled away, he saw the calm upon her.

"There *is* someplace else."

The haze of his kiss cleared, morning fog dispersing under the sun's rays.

"Where is it?" Belamay balked.

Witon smiled, tweaked her nose playfully, and jumped from the bed.

Rushing about the room, searching frantically for his clothes, he began to explain. "Not very long ago, just before I met you in truth, I began to speak with those who captain my ships."

Among his other holdings, the Count of Lahkrok owned a small gaggle of trade ships, those who traveled the shorter waterways to the other parts of Minra Enra to gather goods only available in those areas. "Often ships are thrown off course by storms, or by failing navigational devices. Aha!"

With this exclamation, he pulled a folded piece of parchment from the inner pocket of the quilted jerkin he wore under his armor.

"And when they are thrown off course…" he continued his prattling as if it had never stopped, even as he gently unfolded the parchment and made his way quickly back to the bed, "… they find things."

He laid the unfurled parchment upon the coverlet before Belamay and pointed a finger at a particular spot.

"They find… places." He spoke with hushed reverence, as if in a house of worship.

Belamay tipped her head, switching her gaze from his enraptured face to look down at what he showed her.

"Is that…" She looked up, back down, "is that… land? A new land?"

"Hah!" Witon tossed back his head. "I do not think it new, only new to us."

Belamay kept her eyes on the raisin-shaped plot of land; for, in contrast to Minra Enra, a pie, it appeared no larger than a raisin. "And you… you want to go… there? And live?"

Witon jumped on the bed, bouncing her and the parchment together, grabbing her hands. "I do. With you."

Belamay stared at him as if staring at a madman. "But… but… how would we live? How would we survive?"

"There is everything there we need."

She stared hard, like a mother at a recalcitrant child. "And how would you know that? You have not been gone from me long enough to have made such a journey. And you had better not have made one without telling me!"

He smiled at her loving reprimand. "I sent an exploration party. Two, in fact. And both reported a land of such abundance, of such beauty, it... I..."

Words failed him and yet, in not saying anything, he said all she needed to hear. She took his hands in hers and the gesture gave him the strength to continue. He brought her hands to his cheek.

"There is everything we could ever possibly need and more, much, much more."

"And we would live there alone, just the two of us?" Belamay tipped her head to the side, one eyebrow rising. "I love ye with all my heart, Witon, but I think I would desire someone else to talk to." She wrapped the sheet around her chilling body as she rolled her eyes. "Now and again, at least!"

Witon threw his head back and laughed, then grabbed her head and kissed her hard.

"Though you are all I would ever want or need, no, it would not be only for us. I'm hoping... well, it is my dream that some from every species on Minra Enra would want to join us."

Belamay laughed now as well. But quickly stopped, all amusement melting off her features. "You are serious?"

"Oh yes, quite."

"But… how?"

Witon drew his hands down her throat, down her breasts, caressing her with his fingertips, the slightest of touches. "I want to build a new world, Belamay. I want to find those who, like me, want no more war, no more hate. I know they are out there. I just have to find them."

Chapter VI

A MARRIAGE...OF SORTS

He spent at least part of every day in the room. Witon stayed beside the bed of the recovering creature, talking, until the patient could no longer continue, till he faded into healing slumber. But each day the time grew longer; each time their bond grew stronger.

"Tell me of your life, Persky." He couched a gentle request, made with the familiarity of having spent four whole days together.

Witon had learned the Elf lad's name on the first, but since then had only discussed such things as literature and the strange tales of their land, of Witon's life, his parents, and his family's rise to prominence, descendants of a line of the earliest settlers of Minra Enra. Witon even told him of his eyes and the myth that there was once a Centaur among his ancestors, one so powerful that at least one child of each generation was born with the silvery eyes of the species.

"My brother, Mitren, has always been jealous of them." Witon chuckled fondly at the thought of his only brother. "I remember this one time, we were young, no more than four or five. He... he tried to push mud in my eyes, to turn them brown, like his." Witon shook his head as loving laughter rang deep within his voice. "I had no dinner that night."

Persky's slanted eyes stabbed him. "*You* were punished?"

"Oh no! But my father was a very smart man, if of an old way of thinking, and his punishment was... well, it was as hysterical as it was ingenious."

"What did he do?"

"He filled Mitren's breeches with mud and made him sit in it for the rest of the day, even at table. I couldn't stop laughing long enough to get a single bite of food in my mouth."

Witon's laughter boomed freely, harmonizing with Persky's own twittering guffaws; there were few things as binding as laughter entwined. Finally now, on this day, Witon felt he had earned the creature's trust enough to ask about his own life.

"Tell me of Ramarra."

"I am not an Elf." Persky dropped his slanted-eyed gaze at the mention of the Elf city. "Neither am I Human."

Witon hung in the silent wake of Persky's words. He sat perched on the small stool by the cot in the corner of the room, with his long legs bent wholly in half, knees up near his shoulders; he moved not an inch as he waited.

At length, the creature looked up, his light brown eyes flecked with green. The sadness in them struck Witon as hard as any sword ever had.

"I am neither… and both." A declaration, a confession.

Witon accepted Persky's truth as a gift. He reached out and took a long, thin hand in his. "Your parents?"

Persky shook his still bandaged head. "Both gone, both killed, by their own kind."

Witon's tongue clucked against the roof of his mouth, an ugly sound for such ugly behavior.

"Neither species would accept what they had done." Persky's voice cracked but he gave it no heed. "I have heard that my mother, a Human, was a great beauty, and my father a great thinker. I hope I have a little of both of them in me."

Witon gave no such assurance. They were still too little acquainted for such a declaration; it would have chimed sharply of false flattery.

"How did you survive?"

"My uncle took me in." Persky hitched himself up with his good arm. Witon jumped up from his stool, arranging the pillows so the creature could sit up comfortably. But Persky tried to push him away.

"Ye mustn't, Count e' Lahkrok, 'tisn't proper," Persky protested, his good limb trying ineffectually to wave Witon's attentions off.

"Nonsense," Witon insisted, without a second's hesitation and finished his ministrations. "There is no rank here," he said, retaking his place upon the squat stool, "there is no one species or another. There is only Witon and Persky."

The Elf-Man's wide mouth dropped a bit as his slanted eyes blinked. He dipped his head at the honor bestowed upon him. With a quick glance, Witon could see both geneses in this enigmatic creature; the green of his skin washed pale with human blood; the slight point to his ears, not the sharply angled ones of a pure Elf.

"Besides," Witon said with a chuckle, "I am not a true Count yet, as my father Trilon still lives."

"And may the Stars grant him a long life," Persky replied, with the fine manners of their land.

"You were telling me of your uncle," Witon prompted, as he poured them each a mug of ale from the small table between them.

"Yea, 'twas my father's brother." Persky took a long draught from his mug. A mustache of foam remained behind and he wiped it away with the back of his good hand. "He was a cruel man. He brought me into his home, true, but as a slave. I have served him thus for the whole of my life, all three and thirty years."

"Three and th…?" Witon spewed the small portion of ale in his mouth, dousing them both, grateful for Persky's smile rather than a frown of disgust. "But I am four and thirty. You… you cannot be… what I mean to say is…"

Persky gave a small shake of his head and held up his hand, though it held his mug still. "'Tis true, I assure you. But I cannot explain it to you. They say my father was large even for an Elf, standing close to seven feet at least. My mother, too, was tall for a Human," Persky explained with pride. Though he had never known his parents, the esteem he held them in, for their courage in allowing their love to cross boundaries few ever dared, shone bright in his eyes, in the tender upward curve of his lips. "My uncle claimed my diminutive stature to be a curse, wrought by their indecent love. I say 'tis a blessing."

Witon's brows rose at that. In a land where even Humans grew to great heights, himself standing at six and three, he could not imagine how such a pint-sized anatomy could be a blessing. His confusion must have shown on his face, for Persky answered his question without being asked.

"It has kept me alive, I have no doubt of it," Persky said. "They put me on the front lines, at the strongest points, to lure in whatever enemy they battled. I was their... bait."

Witon struggled for a moment with the truly incomprehensible notion. As the truth of it took hold, as he saw the deep hurt of it in Persky's fair eyes, the anger birthed a monster inside him.

He stood up so fast, the stool tipped over. He spun on booted feet, grumbling over his shoulder, "I bid you to excuse me for a moment."

"Of cour—" Persky began, but Witon had already strode out the door.

* * *

He walked a circle in the large foyer of the manor house, not knowing what to do with himself, with the anger seething inside him. He looked up the curving staircase that would bring him to Belamay and her arms, but Witon felt he had no place within them.

The thudding reached his ears, though they roared with his rushing blood. Witon stomped out the double front doors, marched about the grounds till he found the source.

A stable hand wielded an ax, chopping wood for the house and its many hearths.

Witon almost smiled as he stomped toward the young man, grabbed the sharp tool from the shocked lad's brawny hands, and set to the task himself.

With each thunderous blow upon a stump, as he split and splintered the logs into pieces with such force that they flew from their base, Witon growled and grunted. He cared nothing for the bewildered stare of the young man standing nearby, or those that joined him in audience as Witon's wailings and strikes grew louder and harsher. As sweat dripped from his body, soaking his fine jerkin and hose, he cried out his anger at the unjust world, damning those who had made it so, cursing those who had hurt so fair a creature as Persky.

Witon reached out a hand, the unspoken command for yet another hunk of wood to split, but this time it remained empty.

"There is no more, M'lord," said the young man whose job had been so neatly done for him.

Witon turned then, turned out of himself for the first time since he'd begun, saw those standing around him in a confused bunch, the huge pile of split logs as high as his waist beside him. As it grew, the other diminished, shrank and shriveled away. The anger desperately needing expression had had its say, and not a soul had been hurt, save, mayhaps, for Witon's own back.

He turned the ax, handing it back to the stable hand by the handle, slick with his sweat. "Might I have a cloth or rag, if you please?"

"Of course." The lad took the ax and ran for the stable, returning just as quickly with a cloth, clean but stained with remnants of much use.

"I thank thee, most heartily," Witon said to the youth, wiping his face and hands, turning his depleted body once more for the main building.

"'Tis my… pleasure," the lad said, with great and true enthusiasm.

Witon smiled; why should he not? He'd finished the boy's hardest task of the day. But not Witon's; he had one of great importance left to do.

* * *

Witon entered Persky's room with as little formality as he had left it by.

Persky stirred from a half sleep, roused by the powerful presence suddenly and keenly felt. "I am sorry, My Lord, sorry if I offended—"

Witon stilled him with a hand held up sharply, and crossed the room with a few scant strides, stunning Persky as he knelt by the small bed.

"You have offended no one, my good creature." Witon's voice quivered. "The world has offended you, deeply. I swear to you, I will make it right."

Persky shook his head, pale green skin blossoming with pink. "I... I..."

"If you would do me the honor, I would have ye come live with me." Witon gave him no pause. "Live with me in my home, with my family, become part of our family."

This time Persky would have his say. "Your father would never approve."

"Perhaps not at first." Witon nodded, already thinking how he would broach the subject to the aging and ill Count. But he knew he could not have become the man he was without his father's influence; they shared more than blood, Witon knew it as well as he knew his own name. "But you need not concern yourself with it."

Persky's slanted eyes grew round. His mouth worked, but he said naught.

Witon smiled. "Does that mean you will come?"

Persky nodded. "It would be the greatest pleasure I have ever known to do so."

"Hah! Wonderful!" Witon burst with joy. Grabbing the stool, he drew it closer to Persky's bed and sat once more. "Now, this next request... well, it is not so easily answered and I pray ye will take time before answering."

Again, Persky nodded silently, yet with a perplexed furrow upon the smooth skin of his brow.

Witon began to talk, began to tell this creature of all his political efforts to bring peace to Minra Enra, and finally revealed all he had told Belamay of this new land and his designs for it.

"Amazing," Persky whispered at the end of the story.

"Indeed," Witon agreed.

"But… what it is you wish to ask of me?"

Witon chewed on his top lip. "I ask your help, Persky. I ask ye to come with me to the leaders of each species and see if they wish to be part of this new world of ours." Already, Witon felt its reality… knew it belonged to at least him, Belamay, and Persky; a start.

Now, Persky's skin blanched of all color and he became almost as beige as Witon himself. "Me? You want m… my help? How could I possibly help with such an insurmountable task?"

Witon once more took his hand. "You can tell your story, just as ye told it to me. If there is anything in their hearts that longs for peace, it will be touched by such a tale."

Persky left his hand in Witon's, staring at the pair that looked so different in their skins and their formations, and yet were so similar in so many ways.

Looking up, he smiled, for the first time in a very long time. "I am at your service, My Lord."

Witon grinned, broadly and merrily, gave Persky's hand a squeeze, and, to Persky's utter astonishment, stood and offered the Elf-Man a deep bow. "And I, Good Sir, am at yours." It was how one lord would reply to another.

Seeing Persky's flabbergasted expression, Witon laughed, put one hand on each side of the creature's head, and gave his forehead a hard, smacking kiss.

"Get well, Persky," Witon called over his shoulder as he fairly skipped from the bed to the door. "Get well so we may go home."

"My Lord!" Persky cried, stopping Witon in his tracks.

"You must call me Witon."

Persky nodded. "Witon?"

"Yes, Persky?"

"You will change my life."

Witon sniffed as he smiled, as he gently shook his head. "No, my friend, you will change all our lives."

Chapter VII

HARD WORK WELL DONE

They came and went for a days at a time. Between each foray, there were long days of study... of the city they would next travel to, of the leaders they would next meet. In the sparse spaces between, Belamay was there, sharing intuitive insights—those so often missing from the male mind—ensuring they ate, that both households and land holdings were maintained, hers as well as Witon's.

On particular occasions—more than one—she accompanied them, to the few—too few—cities where the female of the species stood on equal ground with the male.

To the Faerie Dell she led them, though she could have easily left them behind, so unneeded were they. She spoke with the resplendent Faerie Queen quietly, yet a conversation so full and quick, the males present felt like unnecessary ornaments. As the two females laughed, pleasure closed Witon's eyes, but only for a moment. Like Persky, he could not keep his gaze away from the beauty of the Faeries' wee forms.

To the Dwarves' mountain-deep dwellings, the males went on their own, which proved the right decision as, for three whole days, Witon and Persky wallowed in a cold stone room in the village beneath the mountains. For three days, they were ignored by the Dwarf King and were given nothing more than some form of gruel to eat, one neither could name, nor cared to. On the third day, Witon gained consent to explain his quest, his hopes and dreams, but only to an underling, not the king himself. On the third day, they were ousted from the stone prison and from the entire mountain city, and the gigantic stone slab slid quickly closed in their faces.

And yet, like so many a great meal, the final course tasted the sweetest. The Dwarf that came to them, slipping from some secret crevice none but those who lived under the mountain knew, gave them their true just desserts; he pledged his allegiance, and that of more than a few of his species, to their cause; to the hopes of a new world.

To the Lapiths, too, only Witon and Persky went; only the two of them dared to go. It went as expected. Belamay did her part upon their return, treating their wounded bodies and their battered hearts.

* * *

Witon sat by the bedside in a chair so well stuffed, he thought it alive and grasping, holding him in place. Just as well; it gave him somewhere to hang his heavy head.

"What troubles ye, my son?" The croak broke the silence previously punctuated by the ins and outs of the old man's wheezy breathing.

"Hello, Father." Witon smiled. "Good to see you awake."

"You look like the Great Stars have spat upon you, yet 'tis I that am dying."

Witon snorted. "Very kind of you to say, Sir." Somehow, he suppressed the tremor caused by the ease with which his father spoke of his own passing. He stood and fussed about with linens and pillows, until a soft slap landed upon his hand.

"Tell me." No aged warble came forth this time, but a parental command.

We are always children to those who call us child. The thought flashed in Witon's mind and, strangely, brought comfort. But he turned the tables on his forebear.

"Tell me, Father, when you negotiated the trade agreement with the Creevons, what methods did you use?" Witon asked, his voice thick with feigned spontaneity, his features contorted with enforced nonchalance.

Trilon turned his head ever so slightly, the few straggly strands of hair remaining on his head rustling upon the pillow. With his weak voice, a shadow of its former domineering boom, the elder count elucidated diplomacy. As elders tended to do, his tale wandered, but the winding path was a good one for Witon; it meandered to other times when diplomacy was called for, when negotiation and compromise held sway. He drank in his father's words as if they were water and he had not drunk for days. His mind whirled, angles and tactics formulating even as he father continued.

"…is it?"

Witon shook his head. "I'm sorry, Father, I did not hear your question."

"Indeed. I do not think you've heard a word I've said for the last five minutes." Trilon struggled to sit higher upon his pillow. Witon reached out and grabbed his father's arm that still felt so firm despite looking withered.

Upright, cleared-eyed, Count Trilon stared at his eldest offspring. "What are you on about, my son?"

The fear came upon him all of a sudden, without invitation or behest. Witon was as frightened as he had been when, as a small boy, he had 'borrowed' his father's favorite bow, managing not only to accidentally kill one of his father's prized falcons, but to break the bow in the killing as well. And yet, he pushed the fear aside, saw within the darkly smudged, sagging skin, the warm golden brown eyes that had beamed so much love upon Witon's shoulders, warming them as if a hot sun beat its glow on them. Witon inhaled deeply... and told.

Silence met his tale; in it, his childish fear crept back, scurrying into the recesses of his heart, only to be broken on his father's soft chuckle.

"You... are your mother's child." Trilon coughed a bit as his chuckle turned to a laugh.

Witon blinked silver eyes arrhythmically, till the skin around them crinkled; till he joined in the laughter, pure, delighted mirth. "And why is that, Father?"

"She was a dreamer, too, but a dreamer who could put purpose to her hopes. We wouldn't have been half so successful, and merciful, were it not for her."

Witon closed his eyes, overwhelmed by a flood of memories, of the beautiful woman with long wavy hair flowing to her waist, the woman who dressed as a pirate with him, who ran barefoot around the castle with him. Too soon they had lost her, when Witon had barely reached young adulthood, but she lived still and forever in their hearts, perhaps even more than Witon thought. If her tutelage had given him his capacity for wanting more—wanting better—and his determination to make it happen, she would be the grandmother of a new world, magnificent with its peaceful innovation.

"Then... you approve?" Witon asked, but even to his own ears, his voice sounded like that of the five-year-old he'd once been, hopeful for consent.

Trilon simply smiled, moved an age-spotted hand from the bed to cover Witon's own, and gave it a squeeze, the best he could manage.

* * *

"It's amazing, Belamay, he actually approves! He did not chastise or rail or call my plan disastrous."

"What *did* he say, my love?" Belamay prodded, eyes wide, sparkling in her lover's glow.

"He... he said I was my mother's son."

With a small chirp, Belamay hid her awed smile with her hand, while with the other she brushed his stubble-covered cheek. Grabbing her hand, he put the soft palm to his lips as he wished silently, *Oh Mama, how I wish you could meet her. How much you would love her.*

* * *

"I must see My Lord Witon immediately." The demanding voice did its best to out-clamor the clang of armor just outside the study door.

Before Witon could jump from his chair to see what was amiss, the door burst open. In the doorway stood his sergeant at arms, Fosrin, armed and armored for battle, face cruel and hard with a coming fight.

"Fosrin, what has—"

"The Lapiths engage the Centaurs, My Lord." Fosrin barked the answer before hearing the whole question. "We must muster and make our way to Cremora."

Hands up and splayed, Witon encouraged calm. "Wait, Fosrin. Slow down, if you please. Come, sit down." He gestured toward his treasured desk and the velvet chairs before it.

Fosrin tossed away Witon's courtesy. "There is no time, My Lord. We cannot allow the Lapiths' control to spread any farther. I have no care for the Centaurs, as I know you don—"

"I fight no longer."

The meager, potent words stopped the weathered soldier as no well-placed sword had ever dared. Fosrin stumbled a step, two, backward.

"You will not...?" His hard voice, now muddled, trailed off into confusion, his fine features scrunching cruelly.

"I am set upon another course." Witon's words cracked in the tight air. "I can no longer be an instrument of death."

He stood and leaned forward. Though he again gestured a hand to the chairs before him, Fosrin only took a few steps closer, not even casting a glance towards a seat.

Witon dropped his head, his silver eyes scurrying across the mess of letters and maps amassed upon the desktop. "I'd planned to come to ye soon, in a day or two at most, to ask you to join us."

In a manner appropriate to a seasoned military man, Witon told Fosrin all. Barely into his tale, he glimpsed a mien of disgust on Fosrin's face, the likes of which Witon had never beheld in all the battles they had fought together.

"You are leaving Minra Enra?" Fosrin tipped his head slightly askew as if the ear on that side had failed to work properly. "You will live... live side by side with..."

Witon smiled. He could not help it when so many, if not all, had finally committed to the cause. "With Dwarves and Centaurs and Faeries and Brownies and, possibly even—"

"Dwarves?" Fosrin spat, a hand moving to the hilt of his sword. "And B-Brownies?"

Witon's eyes narrowed to slits. He knew Fosrin's beliefs were deeply rooted in the segregation of the species—in the prejudice of a species hierarchy—but Witon had never realized the depth of the man's hatred; hatred of creatures he had never spoken a word to, had only raised a sword against. Here lay the greatest symbol of the evil infesting this land, one long embedded and inbred.

"You will remove your hand from your weapon…" Witon leaned forward, hatred snarling in his gut, tight fists braced on his desk, "… or I will kill you with it."

Fosrin snarled; he moved not an inch.

"You are a traitor!" Fosrin spat. He did moved then; he moved his hand to the crest upon his chest, the Alerion perched on the branch of a Beech set upon a background of wavy lines of dark and light green… the coat of arms for the Lahkrok nobility, Witon's nobility, and yanked.

The crest, edges frayed and torn, dropped to the floor, as did any bond between these men.

Silver eyes pierced the man before him; it took great consciousness to control his breathing, the heart hammering in his chest. "You will remove yourself from my property, never to return."

Fosrin stared back with all the bigotry infesting his heart and mind.

"GET OUT!" Witon screamed, fury unloosed, hand thrust out with a condemning, pointed finger.

Walking backward, Witon locked in his sights, Fosrin moved. "I will see your end."

Witon laughed; not a single pleasant note rang in the sound.

"You will see naught more than the back of my ship as I leave you and all like ye behind… forever."

"I will fight on, I promise you." Fosrin stood at the door even as guards filled the hallway behind him, alerted by the ferocious scream of the young count.

Witon nearly jumped over his desk, he moved around it so fast. "You will not do so with any of my men or you will feel my sword in your gullet."

Now, Fosrin took his turn to pretend a laugh. "Do you really think all your men will stand beside you… that they will take part in this disgusting quest of yours?"

Witon felt his teeth grind as he slammed his mouth shut. He had never thought of it, never considered that there could be members of his dominion who would not want the life he wanted. But of course there would be; his own naiveté appalled him.

"You will leave that to me. I will tell them, I will ask them. Any who do not wish it, I will send to you."

Fosrin smirked with ill-gotten victory.

"And you may all rot in the darkness of the Starless realm together."

The curse, so eagerly plied, the worst in the land, did its work. Fosrin left the castle on fleeting feet.

* * *

They could not help themselves; they had to know, had to see.

Witon, Belamay, and Persky watched the battle from the outskirts.

They sat upon their horses, perched upon a rise above the shallow valley where all manner of creatures butchered each other in a barbaric battle worse than any these three battle-weary beings had ever seen. It seemed as if the combatants were determined to create a river through the gulley between the low hills; a river of bodies and blood. The screams of death rose up to the onlook-ers like specters from a grave, and they shivered at the bleakness.

With tears running down his cheeks, Witon pulled on the reins of his horse and turned away from the battle still rampant below.

"I can see no more."

* * *

He slept in fits and starts, the battle raging over and over in his mind, the sights and sounds a constant clatter in his unconscious.

Witon woke with a startled jerk, crashing into aware-ness by Belamay's harsh gasp.

He looked up at her, rubbing his eyes against the light of dawn. "What, Belamay, what is it? Are you hurt?"

Belamay shook her head, her long, sleep-tangled hair swooshing about her, her mouth a thin line across her pal-lid face. Without word or warning, she rushed from the room, returning in seconds with a reflective glass the size of a portrait, snatched from the hallway wall, and held it before Witon.

He knew not the man staring back at him. Through the course of the night—as he slept and dreamt, dreamt of war and killing and death—every strand of Witon's golden-brown hair had turned pure white.

Chapter VIII

SIGNS TELL OF THE TIMES

The black iron gates rose up before them, almost as tall as the Dwarves' mountain and nearly as beautiful. Scrolled and twisting, almost delicate in their impassability, they commanded those who came to them not only to stop, but to stare and admire.

Witon gave their names to one of the guards, along with his request to meet with the Elvin lord. As the soldier trundled off, running up the long, winding pathway—a swath of grayish pink pebbles through a kaleidoscope green forest—Witon and Persky sat atop their mounts and waited.

The guard returned, the gates opened as eight Elves pushed them, four to each side, and Witon's breath quivered in his chest.

He turned to his stalwart companion—a greater one no Man had ever been blessed to have beside him. "This is the one, Persky. The one that could change it all."

Persky's lips stretched tight across his sharply angled face, nerves of many different colors pulling them so, nodded. "Indeed it is."

With that, they snapped their reins, clipped their heels into their horse's flanks, and entered Vamarra, the great Elvin city, the largest city on all of Minra Enra.

* * *

"Belamay! Persky!" He ran through the house, waving the parchment roll in his hand as if he were a wizard and the roll his mighty wand. "Persky! Belamay!"

His excited voice echoed hollowly through the castle which, though made of hard stone, radiated warmth, its walls rich with thick tapestries, man-sized fireplaces in every room and fresh rushes on the floors, replaced every day.

"Where are they?" Witon muttered, but not without a smile. His joy infected him, enveloped him. The news on the parchment came as an answer to a prayer, as if the Stars blessed him and all his dreams and hopes. He needed them, the two who had worked tirelessly beside him all these months to make it happen; needed desperately to share it with them.

He took the stairs two steps at a time. Perhaps they were both in their rooms, both napping. But as he burst into Belamay's sitting room, then Persky's small chamber, shaking his head at the creature's refusal to use a more luxurious room, he found both vacant.

Witon stood in the hall, whirling round as his mind spun with the possibilities of their whereabouts, scratching his head, creating even more disarray of his disheveled gray locks.

56

That's when the door to his father's room opened and Belamay stepped out. That's when Witon saw her beautiful face ravaged by sadness, stained with tears. That's when he knew.

With no conscious thought, he dropped the parchment and ran, down the hall, past Belamay, and into the master's chamber.

The smell hit him, as did the shroud of darkness. The shutters stood closed to fresh air, the curtains drawn against any light. In the shadows, he saw Persky huddled small on a chair in the corner, eyes moist with tears, rising as Witon entered. By the bedside, the great Medical Advisor, Hervay, stood. He did not administer to the patient; he simply stood beside him. Seeing Witon, the physician stepped back with a hand to his chest, bowing his head with a closing of his eyes.

But Witon did not move, did not enter the room; in his mind, he ran—ran from the truth, the truth of this moment. Until the shaky hand rose up from the linens… till it reached toward him.

With a sob, he flew to his father's bedside, grabbing the weak limb with both of his strong hands and holding it against his cheek.

"How goes it, Father?" Witon swallowed back his tears, almost choking on their need to be spilled, even at the sound of his father's wheezy chuckle.

"It goes no longer, my son." Trilon's eyes fluttered, barely opened; as if the weight of his lids was too much for him. "Your mother calls to me at last, and I am ready to heed her beckoning."

The words broke him. Witon dropped his head to the ticking his father lay on, pushing his head into the crook of his father's arm as if he were once again the little boy whose whole body fit there. "I will be lost without you."

"Nonsense," the count sniffed, with the strength of the man he once was, with his conviction of the rightness of his final journey. "You are the best of us, the strongest of us. You will do more than we could ever have imagined for you."

Witon looked up. Such words of love and affection did not come easily to the staid nobleman, one never overly comfortable with displays of emotion.

"Does it go well... y... your project?" the count asked on a wheeze.

Witon rolled his eyes, almost smiling at the thought that his father would care, even in this moment, about his son's efforts. It had always been that way, whether the count would admit to it or not.

"It goes very well, Father." Witon nodded, both hands unmoving, clenched tight to his father, as if the hold could keep the Great Stars from doing their work this day. "In fact, it goes so well that the Elves... or a part of them... have agreed to join us."

Belamay squeaked. Persky sucked in his breath. The count smiled.

"I leave it to ye, all of it, the entirety of my fortune." The count squeezed his son's strong hands with the last bit of strength left in them. "No conditions. Do whatever it is you need to do with it."

Witon could not speak, could not find words. His father's last gift was freedom… the permission to give it all up, to leave this world behind without regret or remorse, without guilt over dismantling the family heritage that had been centuries in the making. It was never done, this unqualified giving; on Minra Enra, the continuity of power meant everything, even in death.

He took his father in his large arms, held him still and fast, long after the last breath left the man's body.

* * *

They had all come and gone, paying their respects to the dead nobleman, more than a few offering words of warning to the new one. Even as he laid his father in the cold ground, they dared to divest him of his intentions. He scalded them with a burning glare.

At last, only the four of them remained. Witon stood with Belamay under his arm, holding him up. His brother, Mitren, younger by a few years, stood close by his other side. And Persky positioned no more than a step away.

As the spring breeze caught hold of his hair, Witon closed his eyes and held his face up to the caress. When it passed, he knew.

"It's time," he told them. "I will leave this kingdom of hatred and I will take all those who wish a better life with me."

Chapter IX

THE LAST LASTING TOUCH

He rolled over, facing her and the wall of windows. No light save that of the moon shone through the slats of the shutters, its silvery beams touching her body in spots and sputters. He followed them downward, from her round face so peaceful in slumber; yet somehow, even in sleep, the pink blush kissed her porcelain cheeks. Witon's gaze traveled through the tangle of raven curls gathering in the hollow of her long neck and about her bare shoulders. His breath caught as it found those rays fortunate enough to fall upon her bountiful breasts, to dip into the valley of her slim waist, and rise again in glory to her rounded hips.

He chuckled as he felt himself grow hard just looking at her, though he had been doing so for so long. His whispered laughter caught in his throat.

When will I look upon this marvelous creature again?

Such a worry he could not deny; a sadness that pinched him far too often. Witon knew the Stars had truly blessed him with this woman who gave of herself so freely, without any bans or bonds, just the truth of what burst and shone between them. He remembered the day he had seen her on the battlefield, so strong, so fierce. He had never seen a woman warrior before; there were so few who dared defy convention and leave themselves open to such ostracism as she most surely encountered. It showed him the truth of her courage, far beyond that of any other creature he knew. He had known love in that instant—and lust—unlike any he had ever experienced.

The lines of light found skin; Belamay's leg had escaped the linens and sat atop them. Witon followed the lights willingly, down to the small dollops of her toes. She gave a soft moan in her sleep as if she felt the stroke of his gaze. It was his undoing.

He began where his eyes finished. Sitting up slowly, linens falling in a bunch about his naked hips, Witon moved to the foot of the bed and took the revealed limb in his hands. With a fluttering touch, as soft as the skin they fondled, his fingertips flickered along her toes, to her ankle, and up her calf. She moaned again and her skin rippled with gooseflesh. He excited her, even as she slept, and it excited him all the more. His penis throbbed harder with the need of her, but he would keep it wanting. This night—this moment—was their last time together… the last time before he sailed away on his dreams, their dreams. Witon would make the most of this moment.

Squirming gently between her legs, turning her onto her back with exquisite slowness, his hands languished up her thighs, one on each, first along the outside curve, then upon the silkiness of the inside. Witon closed his eyes, swallowing hard against the feel of flawless flesh. Ever so slowly, he eased her legs apart; ever so gently, he pulled the sheet from her body. His breath froze at the sight of her revealed perfection.

Witon's eyes roved from her curl-covered mound, its pink lips peeking out at him, to the smooth hollow of her stomach, to the hills of her breasts with hardening tips.

As he leaned his own naked body forward, one hand snaked up to the thatch between her legs—teasing flicks, gentle circlings—while his tongue, touching down upon her stomach, languished up her flesh to her breasts. His fingers found her wet and he almost came himself then, so titillated by what he did to her. His tongue brought her nipples ever harder, and he closed his eyes as he lapped at them, as he teased them softly with his teeth.

"Please, Witon, I can take no more."

His eyes popped open and up, to find her awake. Awake and watching, features softened yet tight with need.

Witon laughed softly as he moved his mouth from her breast to her mouth, as his tongue swirled around her lips, then in and out of them. Her legs came up and wrapped around his body; their strength pulling him closer, demanding he enter her.

He did as she bade and they both groaned with the pleasure of it. With all the control he had learned on the battlefield, Witon only allowed the head of his penis to enter, to flick in and out, for the thick ridge of him to flick the lip of her. She arched her back, her neck, pushing against him, and he laughed again at her need.

But he forgot what a warrior she was. She parried.

Curling forward, shoulders rising up, Belamay's hands reached out and down between their slick bodies, one taking the portion of his still exposed shaft, the other his tight sack just beneath. She stroked one as she gently squeezed the other.

The arms holding him above her trembled; Witon grunted against a wave of desire that threatened to fell him, that stiffened his entire body with bursting need.

"Now, Witon, now." She breathed her lust as if it were a thing he could touch; she rocked her body to a rhythm demanding a dance. He answered.

Without restraint he plunged, he plundered and battered himself home, till he could feel the tip of him pound the tip of her.

Together they cried out; together they released and burst, as did a star newly born.

Chapter X

THE FIRST STEP OF MANY

The screech-like cry of the seagulls rent the air.

"They laugh at me," Witon remarked acerbically, shading his eyes with his hand as he followed the flight of the ocean fowl above the glittering sea.

"No, My Lord, they send ye a bon voyage," said Persky, looking up at Witon, the adoration blatant in his slanted eyes.

The sun sparked off the ocean, the wind playfully nipping at it, making small, lively waves upon its surface. The pungent, briny scent of it invaded Witon's nostrils and his adrenaline soared with the promise of the quest.

He stood at the very edge of the long dock, unable to move his gaze from the beautiful vessel bobbing gently upon low waves.

"She's not big, sir, but she's quite beautiful," Persky said as if reading Witon's mind.

Witon turned his dazzling smile to the small creature. Choosing Persky as his first mate was one of the easiest decisions Witon had ever made.

They made an interesting sight standing together; one fairly small, the other slightly more than six and three, but in each burned the same loyalty... to each other and the beliefs and dreams that bound them.

Witon turned his smile back to the ship his father's legacy had helped to build. The sailing craft, a three-masted schooner about one hundred and twenty-five feet long, was constructed of mostly square timbers. The ship's design served multiple purposes; to bring them to their destination, to return and guide the second ship onward, and, once there, to be dismantled and the wood used to erect temporary housing in their new world.

"A new world," Witon intoned, as if he prayed.

"You have never looked at me so longingly." The soft, seductive feminine voice broke Witon's contemplation. With a hearty chuckle and a hitch in his breath at the recollection of last night's perusal of her, he turned to see his Belamay approaching, resplendent in her form-fitting purple bliaut, the gold chain resting on her hips marking their sensual sway.

"My longing for you is always here." He placed a hand upon his heart. Leaning down, he brushed his lips upon hers, his eyes never leaving her bright face, one he swore looked more beautiful than the day he had first seen it.

Where would I be without her?

Belamay reached up and pushed a stray strand of white hair from Witon's face. He felt her gaze warm upon his cheeks. Pulling back, but only a smidge, she laughed with almost comic delight.

"Do I amuse you so?" Witon did his best to look brutish; smoothing any smile from his sun-drenched skin, forming a straight line with his full lips. A futile attempt.

"Your eyes are aglow like a boy's, one ready to grab a sword for the first time," Belamay chortled.

Her laughter died away and in her pitch-dark eyes, Witon saw what he felt, the heartbreak of leave-taking.

"It will not be long, I swear it to you," Witon said as if reading her mind. "If the maps are correct, we shall reach land in just four days. As soon as we do, I shall send the ship back to lead yours."

"If the maps are correct... if you don't encounter a storm... if..."

"If you worry so much, you cannot see to our work." Witon entwined her arm in his and led her to the edge of the dock. "I need you to reassure the others, keep them from changing their minds. They will feel the same fear as you. You must keep them strong."

Belamay commanded what they called the ship of love, for when the first vessel made land, they would follow, the families of those who charted the course, who dared go before all others, into the unknown. She would bring their loved ones and, with them, the new land would be full of the love required for a world to be born.

She shook her head with a smile and Witon knew she shook off her fears. She became, once more, that fiery, ferocious warrior he had met on the battlefield.

"I will keep myself, and them all, strong." Belamay squeezed his arm.

In tune as always, their twin gazes danced out upon the sea, pulled out to the ocean's horizon.

"Look, Bel, do ye see it?" His voice came as naught more than a whisper, a faint breeze.

Belamay strained her eyes to search the gently undulating water.

"See what, Witon?"

"Our future," he said, gifting her with his dazzling smile. "I see our future free of hatred and bigotry, a peaceful and serene life, where we can raise dozens of children without constant worry, without losing them to endless battles and war."

Belamay's jaw dropped, unhinged, her eyes popped, bulging.

"D... dozens?" she croaked, shooting a sly look from the corner of her eyes.

Witon gave her hip a slight nudge with his.

"Tease," he chirped, delighted.

Witon turned and raised the hand he held in his. With his gaze locked upon hers, he lifted the cuff of her glove, and, with the softness of a feather's caress, brushed his lips on the underside of her wrist where the skin was thin and the blood rushed so close to the surface. "We will have as many children as you wish, my dear."

He smiled as he watched her skin ripple with pleasure.

"Now who is the tease?" she said, her voice low and husky.

"We will have to..."

"My Lord, My Lord!" Persky ran toward them, calling loudly, waving his arms. "They're coming!"

Witon's eyes popped; he squeezed the hands in his.

"They're coming!" Witon whispered, his voice prayer-like once more. With a parting squeeze of his lover's hands, he spun round to follow Persky.

Belamay smiled as she watched him hurry away. No longer the seductive rogue, but a boy again, Witon shimmered, brilliantly alive with the promise of what lay ahead. She quickened her own step. This historic moment would not happen without her.

* * *

The majestic horses, caparisoned and resplendent with fringed saddle pads and jewel-studded headstalls, stopped at their masters' command. In one graceful movement, the riders dismounted and handed the reins to the sailors on the pier.

Witon approached the two creatures with the greatest of reverence. If not for their support, their acceptance of Witon and his plan for a new world, so many of the other species would have turned him away... would not have followed the lead of the highly regarded species. They were the brothers Nevod and Lydan, two of the greatest Elvin warriors in all history.

"'Tis beginning." Nevod, the older of the two, walked toward him, grasping and shaking Witon's hand, shaking the Human's whole body. Both brothers were large, two of the largest Elves Witon had ever encountered. Physically, both stood no more than half a hand below the towering

Witon; Nevod perhaps a smidge more. Yet they were both larger than life.

With the deep honey-green eyes of the Elvin royal line, they were elders, but not ultimate rulers of the mysterious Elvin Empire. Nevod, aggressive and quick to speak, never hesitant or afraid, had led the Elves to many a victory.

With a deep and empathetic concern for other living creatures, Lydan was a talented and powerful negotiator; his words at the bargaining table resounded always with truth, instilling the utmost trust in all he met.

Together, these two created one of the most powerful living forces in Witon's world; their skills and talents perfectly balanced each other's and their undying loyalty and reciprocal love had kept them together for the whole of their lives, lives now spanning perhaps hundreds of years, though they appeared no older than Witon.

"It would not be happening without you and your brother." Witon returned Nevod's warm greeting, truth bubbling from him in the wide smile and the merest hint of a squeak in his low voice.

"Not true, Sir." Lydan reached out a hand to him. "You are the spark upon which this fire feeds. We are in your debt."

Witon blushed, dropping his gaze humbly. "You are most kind, Sir."

These brothers, these magical creatures, had immediately come to mind once Witon's plan became more than a thought, but an action. But, as he had confessed to Belamay, he was so intimated by their reputations—their very species—that he'd spoken with little grace upon his short visit to Vamarra. He had departed frustrated with himself, feeling sure the Elves would never allow him to return.

In the end, they had come to him.

Witon believed, as did many others, that Elves were more than merely magical creatures; they were the essence, the very amalgamation of magic and spirituality, one so refined that their actual bodies had evolved to a less dense form, gifting them with movement on a higher plane than Humans and other creatures. Some said they could fly, or pass through solid objects. It was even rumored they could shapeshift. No one but the Elves themselves knew; they were a private species whose lives revolved around Nature, its cycles, and their families.

"The Stars have blessed us with a perfect day," Nevod said, closing his eyes, turning his roundish face up to the sun, and breathing deeply. Witon flinched, squinted, certain he saw the creature's body swell with the fresh air it inhaled. When Nevod opened his eyes, he offered Witon a knowing smile. Witon could but stare at him, at the strange eyes, the long, straight hair with its streaks of both black and blond, the long goatee of similar coloring hanging from his lighter green skin in a single long curl, a corkscrew come to life upon his face.

"I think ye speak true, brother," Lydan piped up, turning his lithe body in slow steps to face the four winds. His dark-honey-colored hair lifted as the breeze caught it. An outward sign of his fastidiousness, he wore it tightly bound in numerous dreadlocks which hung almost to his waist.

Belamay stood quietly to the side, giving no thought to the tears welling in her eyes. A movement on her left caught her attention and she glanced over to find a young Human female working a shaft of coal furiously upon a large parchment. Belamay's face split wide with a smile.

The artist, Katrin by name, had been hired by Belamay herself, as a gift to Witon. Katrin would document, with her extraordinary drawings, this most auspicious event. At first, Katrin had been hesitant to accept the commission, leery at the thought of an exploratory sea voyage. But her support of the freedom movement, and the opportunity to be the one to record it, had overcome her fears.

Belamay skipped with pleasure to the woman's side and gasped at what she saw. In just a few strokes, Katrin had quickly sketched Witon and Lydan shaking hands while Nevod stood between them, one hand on each of their shoulders.

"A magnificent place to begin," Belamay softly praised.

Katrin turned and answered her with a shy, satisfied smile.

"Will you be greeting the entire Council?" Belamay heard Lydan ask Witon. "Or do you need to be aboard?"

It had been Lydan's idea, to create the group now called the Council of Creatures, an assemblage of representatives from each species who wished to be a part of this new world and the first of their kind to make the journey to it.

"No, no." Witon shook his head, hair flying about. "I will stand here until the very last creature is on board. We have hired only the best of crew and I know they will prepare the ship for our departure far better than I."

"Then, if you don't mind, we would like to stand with you."

Witon could feel the heat of pleasure upon his cheeks.

"That would be wonderful."

For the next hour and a half, the three colleagues stood shoulder to shoulder, greeting the rest of the group; for the members of the Council of Creatures were arriving.

Chapter XI

THE HANDS OF CHANGE

Their prodigious, magnificent forms became visible as soon as their large hooves took a single step upon the dock.

Witon knew, without benefit of a looking glass, the blaze of wonder upon his face, shining always at the sight of a Centaur. Half-Human and half horse, these creatures were powerful and intimidating beings, beautiful in their majesty. He took a deep, steadying breath, willing himself to play the role of idealistic coordinator—a moniker he had given himself, one he thought defined his role.

"Welcome, Chiron, Chalene." As gracefully as he could, Witon bowed while looking up, making the eye contact so important to these stately creatures. Yet, as silver eyes met silver eyes, there came that shiver, that quiver of familiarity he felt whenever he was in a Centaur's presence. It was the only clue to the truth of the myth of him, but he held fast to it.

When the Centaurs had agreed, had embraced his dream with all the passion he himself possessed, Witon had thanked the Stars for their blessing. Theirs was not only a powerful race but an ancient one, known for peace. With Witon's assurance that the Lapiths were not to be a part of the new world he dreamed of, it solidified the Centaur nation's participation. The Lapiths, a greedy and cruel clan of Humans, lived just to the north of the Centaur realm. They waged constant war for control over the Centaurs, to bring them under Lapith control.

But never, in all his dreaming, would he imagine these two beings as their species' representatives. Siblings, and two of the most powerful of their clan, they were second only to their father, Ixion, who ruled.

"Thank you, Witon." Chiron's voice boomed like cannonfire, a poor reflection of his temperament; his reputation as a just and kind individual was widely known.

Chalene smiled at Witon, turning a studying eye to the vessel she was about to board. "I finally see it and yet, in my heart, I still cannot believe this is about to happen."

"It is, good creature, it truly is," Witon assured her. "I hope you will like the special accommodations we have created for you."

"Any place where I can stretch my legs will be sufficient," Chiron replied, a mischievous grin on his lips. All who heard laughed, naturally. Sufficient legroom for a Centaur was a monstrous undertaking, but the ship's designers had miraculously erected a space, if not an actual cabin, at the stern, allowing the Centaurs to sit and stretch while keeping them covered from inclement weather.

With a nod of thanks, the creatures ascended the plank—one at a time, least they crack it in half—and with but a few steps were aboard. The schooner rocked with their added weight and came to rest with a decided lean to the port, the side both Centaurs presently occupied.

"One on each side, if you please," came a cry from high above. All below turned their gaze upward, finding Mitren, Witon's brother, perched in the crow's nest far above.

Witon's younger and only brother, Mitren believed in his brother's philosophies. More importantly, he believed in his brother. Hoping for nothing more than a peaceful land upon which to become a gentleman farmer, Mitren accepted the position of boatswain with the promise of such a reward, and to stay by his brother's side. They were the only family each of them had; they would hold tightly to each other.

With a smile of understanding and a wave of acquiescence, the Centaurs split apart, balancing the ship once more.

"I don't believe we will cause the same conundrum."

A small but no less determined voice startled the welcoming trio, spinning them round, revealing a sight any male, no matter the species, would find glorious to behold; one of the most beautiful feminine forms any had ever seen, and one of the smallest.

"Very true, Your Highness," Lydan bowed, as did the two beside him, "and how blessed we are with your presence."

Vishena, the ruling Queen of the Faeries, fluttered toward and around the Elf's head. Her bountiful mane of red hair swirled with her, above her and almost to her feet. In an emerald green gown that draped in swathes about her curvaceous body, her deep green eyes sparkled with delight as she studied Lydan's handsome countenance. Her transparent wings fluttered behind her, a bit faster.

"Not yet out to sea and already a beautiful view." Vishena laughed huskily as Lydan blushed. A Nymph Faerie, whose bodies nearly matched those of Humans in shape, although they were much smaller, she was, like most of her kind, startlingly lovely. "Do you not you agree, Flerial?"

"Indeed, Majesty," her companion, almost as beautiful, pale and delicately fair, agreed with contrasting bashfulness. It was, perhaps, the first time the Faerie had seen an Elf, let alone one as handsome as Lydan. Oreads, a genus of Nymph Faeries, were an often shy but always passionate race, naturally drawn to those of Human origin, loving them with ease.

The Faeries' quick agreement to join the Council and the cause came as no surprise to Witon. They were possibly the most exploited of creatures. Small and relatively defenseless, they were prey to many ruthless species; some found them to be an epicurean delight, others sold them to serve as pets, or worse. To have the Queen herself make the first journey astonished many, Witon included. Though her entire realm favored the quest, Vishena would not allow others to take a risk she would not accept herself. Always by her side, came the famed Flerial, known throughout all of Minra Erna as a talented healer.

Spinning once more about Lydan, Vishena twirled to Flerial, gathering her in her wake, and the tiny sprites fluttered to hover before the handsome face of Witon.

"Permission to come aboard?" Vishena asked, smile wide and bright.

Witon laughed, holding up an open his palm to them.

"With the greatest of pleasure, Your Highness." Witon could feel the warmth of their bodies spreading from his hand, up his arm, and into his very being.

Lilting, feminine laughter sounded nearby. He turned to its charming call, finding Belamay and the ship's artist with their heads bent together over the parchment. Belamay dismissed his inquisitive look with a flick of her fingers. This time, Katrin had captured Witon with the two beautiful Faeries on his palm. Belamay laughed at the expression portrayed on Witon's face; the very masculine, aroused look could not be denied, nor could Vishena's enjoyment to have wrought it.

"Make yourselves comfortable, Your Majesty, but please be careful. Once we are out to sea, the crew will move quickly at times. I wish no harm to befall you should ye unknowingly get in their path."

"'Twould be our honor to have Her Highness and Flerial ride with us!"

The call came from on board the ship, from none other than Chiron, shocking everyone as he patted a spot on his broad back, a safe place for the Faeries to perch. The number of creatures who had ridden on a Centaur's back in the last hundred years could be counted on one hand; it was, without doubt, one of the greatest honors their world knew.

"Well, we *are* off to an auspicious beginning, are we not?" Vishena said softly, for Witon's ears alone, and with a slight bow, and Flerial by her side, she flew from his hand to take a comfortable seat upon the great creature.

His pleased smile still in place, Witon turned back to the end of the dock, whereupon the amusement slid off his features like a raindrop from a low-hanging leaf.

"And now we shall see just how auspicious it really is."

The Elves who, apart from himself, were the only creatures close enough to hear, followed his gaze with their own.

Coming towards them were two pairs of creatures who walked side by side; two species which had lived in completed hatred of each other for uncounted millennia.

"Seeing them so close, I never realized…" Witon's voice, filled with wonder, trailed off.

"… how similar they look." Nevod finished his thought succinctly.

"Yes, it… it is so very curious," Witon agreed.

Both species were larger of head than body, with arms and legs disproportionately small for their torsos, causing them to walk with a side-to-side rocking motion. Dwarves were less intimidating at first glance, rounder-faced, with welcoming eyes and plump, pink cheeks. Predisposed to wrinkled skin and gray hair, even the youngest Dwarf tended to look elderly. An endearing countenance that could easily deceive.

Dwarves were suspicious and untrusting, tending to believe the worst from the onset. This very nature kept them estranged from other species, as well as constantly warring with the Trolls.

There were few who were not repulsed by a Troll's appearance. Their large stature—taller than the tallest of humans—their skin of black hide bristling with broad, wire-like black hair which, on some, covered the whole of their bodies, suggested a frightening impenetrability. Their full lips seemed forever locked in a perpetual snarl, revealing sharp, fang-like teeth, a glimpse of the darker side some—though few—of the Trolls had embraced.

The worst tended to be poachers who thought nothing of taking what they wanted from whomever had it. This proclivity of disrespect, combined with the Dwarves' suspicious natures, had kept these creatures at odds, the worst of one feeding greedily on the worst of the other.

Yet those who took the time to get to know each species soon learned that both could be extremely caring and lovingly playful. Their appearance this day, each realm's agreement to be part of the new world order taking form, served as an undeniable testament that they, too, had had enough of hatred and war.

Witon watched their approach. Had they spoken to each other? Would they? The answer could mean the success or failure of the entire mission.

Perhaps his imagination allowed him to see that which he wished to see, but it appeared to Witon that, as the foursome came before him, the Trolls held back, allowing Witon to greet the Dwarves first.

He shook the male Dwarf's hand with enthusiasm. "Swerin, good sir, welcome, welcome."

"Glad, I am, to be here," the Dwarf, in mid-life, like his partner, his wife Jwara, nodded repeatedly. "She's a beauty." He lifted his other hand, the one holding a large carpet bag, and waved it toward the ship. The contents of the bag jangled merrily.

A talented metallurgist, as were most male Dwarves, Witon knew Swerin laid claim to high hopes for what he might accomplish when not forever forced to craft weapons of destruction. Jwara, an herbalist, had been schooled in the old ways of growing and breeding healing plants by her mother and her mother's mother. No doubt *her* large satchel overflowed with such remedies. She dipped a fine curtsey for a body so cumbersome.

"'Tis so very exciting, very exciting indeed," she twittered as she rose. "Will we be leaving soon?"

Witon laughed. Her delight was infectious. "Very soon, my lady."

"Wonderful, wonderful," Jwara chirped, stepping aside to allow the Trolls to be greeted.

Witon gave a hopeful, sidelong glance to the Elves as they made their hellos to the Dwarves. He lifted his hand to the two Trolls, only to have it swallowed, though gently, by theirs, and pumped with fervor.

"A new world, Witon," Uganta, the largest, said.

"A new life," Turatan chimed in.

Just like any other youthful male creatures, the excitement of these young Trolls swaggered in the jaunt of their ungainly steps and the swing of their hairy arms as they turned to meet the Elves.

Greetings made, the four creatures turned, almost as one, to make for the gangplank, one not large enough to allow all four to pass at the same time.

Uganta stopped in his tracks and turned to the Dwarves. Witon and the Elves held their breath.

"After you," he said and, with a wave of his stumpy hand, gestured for the Dwarves to embark before him.

"Can I carry that for you?" Turatan asked of Jwara and, without waiting for a reply, relieved her of her heavy case and casually began his own climb up the plank behind them.

Witon exhaled with a whoosh. Nevod clapped him on the back as Lydan shook his head in wonder.

"Miracles really do happen," he said and together, these three shared a quiet laugh of relief.

"Hey, watch where you're putting those big feet."

Witon spun about but saw no one.

"Ouch!" cried Nevod, pulling up his right ankle and giving it a good rub. Lowering his foot, he saw, as did his two companions, the final twosome to join their party.

Brasher and Climora stood defiantly at the feet of the welcoming committee. Hands on hips and small bundles at their feet, the two Brownies waited impatiently for their greeting.

A proud and fierce race, quick to anger and insult, Brownies were sensitive to their own stature. What Trolls were to Dwarves, Brownies were to Faeries. Never taller than a foot or so, their bodies were formed just as those of Humans and Faeries. But, unlike Faeries, they had no wings, so could not fly. Like Faeries, they were magical beings, although dispensing it much more stingily. Darker of hair and skin, they did not suffer the anguish of the Faeries. Too tough for fodder and too cantankerous of demeanor for pets, Brownies were instead considered great sport for hunting.

"Our apologies." Witon crouched down to greet these two with handshakes as well, their hands to his forefinger. "You are the last to arrive but, as the saying goes, the best is always the last."

"Ah, better!" Climora, the female, responded, with a nod to Nevod and Lydan, her brashness of speech also distinguishing her species.

"Everyone else is here?" The male, Brasher, gazed aboard the ship. "Even the Dwarves and Trolls?"

Witon nodded.

"And... have they tried to kill each other yet?"

Both Brownies had been schooled in the world of politics, law, and ambassadorship in the, as yet, fruitless hope of bringing peaceful coexistence to Minra Enra. It made them the most logical choice to represent their nation.

"On the contrary," Lydan reported happily, detailing with true delight the exchange of just a few moments ago.

Climora gave Brasher a hefty punch in the shoulder.

"Told you," she said victoriously and held out her hand, open palm upward. "Hand it over."

Brasher growled. Reaching into his leather garb, he pulled out what appeared to be a coin, and slapped it into his companion's hand.

"That will be the last you get from me."

Witon laughed, despite his efforts not to; Brownies were well known for their gambling, betting on the least little event. He felt sure it would not be the last coin to pass between their hands.

"Shall we go aboard?" Witon asked of the small group remaining on shore.

With all the members of the Council of Creatures accounted for, they could all take their place on the ship. He turned back to the Brownies first.

"As I mentioned to the Faeries, once we are underway, the crew may need to move quickly. Please take care not to inadvertently get in their way. We wish to keep you safe and unharmed."

There came no offer from the Centaurs like the one made to the Faeries. It was withheld out of respect. A Brownie would consider such an offer an insult.

As the Brownies and Elves began their ascent, a young Man on board gave a shout.

"The tide has turned!"

Witon looked up to see the Purser, Arkan by name, standing at the prow of the ship, studying the ocean below. His pronouncement was perhaps the most important one of the morning; the tide had changed direction, ebbing outward now.

Witon turned to see Belamay helping Katrin pack her supplies. The two women embraced and Katrin rushed aboard. Belamay found her beloved with a sad smile on his lips and a tear blossomed in her eye. Witon opened his arms and she rushed into them.

Separating only slightly, staring deeply into each other's eyes, Witon studied her entire countenance; the mental picture he created would have to last him far longer than ever before. He longed to tell her all that pumped in his heart—of his undying love and devotion, his unwavering fidelity, and his deep gratitude—but the words wouldn't come. He kissed her, deeply, mightily, and took the first, awful step away from her.

"Forever in my heart," he finally said, releasing the tips of her fingers, all which remained in his embrace.

"In my heart forever," Belamay replied and brought those tips to her lips.

With a bouncing stride, Witon boarded the ship. Belamay went to stand along the length of the mainland, surrounded by others who had come to bid family members goodbye. A jaunty wind suddenly kicked up, swirling hair and lifting long skirts as it swhooshed around them. The families on the dock heard the rousing cry from those onboard; a stout wind always hailed an omen for success.

The ropes creaked as the knots were undone. Witon shouted to the Master, the Master to the Boatswain, the Boatswain to the crew. Overhead, the lonesome cry of the seagulls filled the air as the ship pointed its prow out to sea and, with a grunt of effort from the oarsmen, launched.

* * *

Belamay waved to the passengers on board, who looked back at the dock and the last of the world they knew. The grin began to tickle her lips, then grew to a full smile. Before she realized it, she laughed, loudly, merrily. Slowly but surely, the laughter grew around her, swelled to a crescendo.

Sailing out to sea together, waving to those they left behind, was the most miraculous grouping of creatures any had ever seen together. Centaurs and Elves, Dwarves and Trolls, Faeries and Brownies stood alongside Humans as they set off on this amazing adventure, one that could change the very essence of life as they knew it.

Belamay stood on the dock, waving and laughing, until just the very back of the ship could be seen. The morning sun rose to its highest point and its reflection glittered off the gilded letters blazoned across the wood, trumpeting the name of the vessel.

Freedom.

Chapter XII

THE VOYAGE OF THE FREEDOM

He had never felt so small, as if he were no more than a speck of dust in the cosmos. The ship that had once seemed so large, felt minuscule in this infinite space. Miles and miles of dark ocean stretched out around him as far as his eye could see. Above him, a star-filled sky reached down to the rolling waves. Overwhelming quietness and stillness wrapped him in a powerful cloak of warmth and anonymity.

Witon stood at the wheel, guiding the *Freedom* toward their destiny, toward their new home.

The powerful thought thrilled him, stars all his own bursting in his pale silver eyes as they searched the unfamiliar heavens above him. It would be a new world, he would see to it, no matter what the sacrifice; a world where all the myriad creatures of his homeland could live side by side with Humans in harmony. Beneath his feet, beneath these creaking, squeaking wooden planks rubbing against each other as the boat shifted upon the churning ocean, the Council of Creatures slept.

Witon pushed back the long, white strands of hair from his face, reveling in the warm, cleansing wind as it rubbed at his skin; a stout wind to bring them through the night and into their future.

"Let me relieve you, brother." On bare feet, Mitren climbed silently up the stairs to the upper deck. "Ye need to get some rest."

Witon smiled fondly at his sibling, at the dark brown, tousled hair and the sleepy brown eyes.

"I don't know if I can, brother. The magic of this moment stirs my blood. Besides, 'tis still early in the night. You should take some rest first."

Mitren chuckled low in his throat. With a loving touch, he removed Witon's clutching hands from the wheel, replacing them with his own.

"I have already slept for five hours, Witon. 'Tis but an hour or two 'til dawn."

Witon's jaw dropped, tired eyes fluttering as he cast about an incredulous glance.

"Ye jest?"

"Nay. Persky is up already and will take the last Candle Watch." Mitren gestured with a tic of his head toward the stern. There, the thin, pointy-eared Elf lit each sleeping lantern. "There is naught left for you to do but sleep."

Witon shook his head and clapped a large hand on his brother's shoulder.

"Thank ye, Mitren. I will at least lie down and see what happens. Good night to ye."

"Good morn to ye," Mitren said with another laugh, new stars sparkling in his earthy eyes.

Witon made his way below decks and walked along the narrow hallway, passing the closed doors of the other cabins. Some of the strangest sounds he'd ever heard escaped from behind these portals. Behind the polished planks, the creatures snored, and the differences in vocal cords and tones created a strange symphony of slumber, music to Witon's ears.

Rubbing his hands over the smooth walls of the walkway, he inhaled deeply, delighting in the rich odors of mahogany, cedar, and oak. He enjoyed it now for he knew that soon, the pungency of unwashed bodies would eliminate it all together.

Witon entered his diminutive cabin in the pointy bow and, for a moment, stopped before the small mahogany desk that had been a gift from his mother during his school days. Maps and charts, including one depicting the new world awaiting them, already covered the dark red surface. He put his finger on the splotch representing the medium-sized landmass. He held fast, in his mind, to those who had charted it and prayed to the Great Stars that it did, indeed, hold everything required to sustain life, and abundantly so.

The land, raisin-like in shape, ran twice as long as it did wide. It boasted natural ports for healthy trade, plus a profusion of fresh water as well as forests, mountains, and plenty of flat land for farming.

Witon lovingly rubbed the map and the land of their future home as if it were alive upon the foolscap and could feel his caring. He shook his head at his own silliness and threw himself down upon his hammock with a laugh.

I'm not the least bit tired, he thought, *I do not know why I am bothering to lay my head down.*

He closed his eyes nevertheless, visions of the life waiting for him, and all on board, dancing in his head.

* * *

The explosion screeched through his ears and he brought his cupped hands up to shield them. His hands quivered against the cold flesh of his skull. He cracked open sleep-swollen eyes but saw no cabin, no floor or walls. He saw instead only chaos, a battlefield where creatures of every sort ran hither and yon, heedless of any purposeful direction. His nostrils flared against the stench of burning flesh, fur, and hair. Shrieking, sobbing, and the twang of launching arrows filled the hollows between cannon blasts. He turned and there, a decapitated Troll… a screaming, legless Goblin… an eviscerated Elf.

Witon squeezed his eyelids shut, rubbing them with balled fists. He brought his hands down, unfurling them, staring at the sticky, moist blood staining them dark and ruddy brown.

"No." He shook his muddled head, mumbling to himself. "No. The wars are over for me."

The bloodstain marks faded and vanished, an unwanted, unbidden phantom of his previous life.

The second explosion burst upon his ears at the same moment he tumbled from his hammock, a hammock designed to sway with the rolling of the ship. Witon smashed his head on the floor just as he heard the cry of his name from someone up on deck, the panic clear in the strained voice. He sat up, trying to shake some sense into his befuddled and bruised brain. The blinding whiteness of lightning stung his eyes as the crash of deafening thunder plundered his ears.

"Storm." He spoke aloud the accursed word.

Witon jumped up, almost cracking his head once more on the low ceiling. He rushed from the cabin, tripping on the scattered items tossed to the floor, but gained his balance before he fell again.

The hallway was short and the stairs few, but it felt like miles before he reached the upper deck. Witon's body flayed back and forth against the passageway's close walls. Between blasts of thunder, desperate shouts of the crew mingled with the passenger's fearful cries.

Witon's head poked above deck, his skin immediately stung by the brutal, wind-driven rain, his eyes almost closing against the onslaught. His brother and Persky besieged him.

"It came upon us in a flash! We couldn't prepare!" Mitren screamed over the roar of thunder and the blasting wind.

"We're taking on water. The crew can't seem to keep up with it!" Persky cried, choking on the deluge of rain rushing into his open mouth. His pale green eyes bulged from his small head and his ashen green skin had turned a sickly yellow.

Witon scanned the terrifying scene. It was morning, he knew it for a certainty. If the sun showed its face, it would be over the horizon, but it hid behind a veil of darkness, a dark beyond dark. Black clouds filled the entire sky, turning it to a low-hanging, ominous roof. The rain poured out, the water hanging from the bottom of the clouds, a wall of liquid crashing down upon them. All around him, every manner of creature held fast to whatever they could grasp. The boat rocked tumultuously. It took every ounce of strength not to topple over and out of the vessel.

Witon looked up. The crew had managed to pull in the sails but couldn't batten them down. They flapped in the wind from the bottom of the masts like white ghosts hovering just above the deck of the ship.

Witon looked to the side and sucked in his breath—as well as the water streaming down his face—so fast, he spluttered and coughed.

The ocean came to life, alive and angry. The waves rushed at them, one right after the other, many feet above the ship's ten-foot sides from waterline to railing. The raging, surging sea pummeled every being on board, again and again, as it crashed over the sides.

"What do we do, Witon, what do we do?" Mitren screamed.

Witon looked at his brother and saw his own stark fear reflected in the familiar eyes.

"Stay alive."

Chapter XIII

ON LAND, AMONG THE STARS, OR HEAVEN KNOWS WHERE

He woke up coughing, gagging on salty seawater caught in his throat. Rolling off his back, Witon pushed himself up onto his hands and knees and gasped and heaved until he felt he would cough his lungs out of his body. Like a cat gagging out fur, he struggled to bring his breathing under control. Slowly it eased, the pain in his lungs faded, and he sat down hard on the wet sand.

Dreamily, with a sluggish motion, Witon brought his hand up in front of his face. The wet beach sand covered his limb, a strange sort of sand, finely textured and glittering ever so slightly, damp though it was. He rubbed his fingers together and felt the grittiness scratch at his skin.

Witon jumped up and looked down. He stood on land, on a beach. With fearful hesitancy, he looked up and around.

The shoreline stretched north as far as his vision would allow. The strange sand looked sodden, still wet from the rain, blending with the ocean as the waves rushed up to meet it, waves unlike any he had ever seen. Their color so crisp and yet so strange, where violet shades blended with the blue ocean he knew.

On what should have been the smooth surface of the coast, lay a stretch of land dotted and misshapen by the lumps of bodies and piles of broken ship wreckage.

"May the Stars protect us," he whispered.

He couldn't move, could barely breathe. He couldn't think. He knew he must do something, everything, anything, but it felt as if his feet were rooted in the ground. He heard a moan and the small evidence of life spurred him into action.

Witon turned. Beside him, a Human body writhed face down on the ground, covered in tattered yet familiar clothing, long brown strands awash with sand. He rushed to it. With insistent but gentle hands, he turned the body over. One glance at the features, and he could do no more than sit back and allow the tears to flow unfettered down his grimy face.

Mitren opened his eyes, blinking at the sight of his crying brother. With slow-moving hands, he rubbed his own face as if to clear the fog from his brain. "Have I broken one of your toys again?"

Witon's jaw dropped, his mouth gaped empty, then his laughter burst out as his tears continued to flow. He laughed and laughed until the hearty warmth of it echoed along the shore and crept into the line of trees bordering it. Witon laughed and the magical sound awakened the other survivors strewn along the sand.

* * *

They sat together in a circle where the now dry, now powdery, glittery dirt of the beach met tall, speckled grass and trees of deep green, each leaf made up of what looked like hundreds of tiny leaflets. The first sparks of a fire glowed in the middle of a small circle of rocks. Pivoting around the flames, a larger circle of boulders served as seats, boulders of deep, marbled green and purple.

The stormy day had finally, mercifully waned. Through thinning, magenta-tinted clouds, the setting sun hung above the horizon's edge, touching the world below with a pale pink glow.

Witon looked at the battered and bruised creatures beside him and a half smile tickled his lips.

"What could possibly be funny?" asked Brasher from his perch atop a tall tree stump next to Witon, indignation burning from all his six inches of stature.

Witon turned to extend his smile to the dark-skinned, hairy sprite and then to the assembly at large.

"I could never have imagined the first meeting of the Council of Creatures would take place under such bizarre conditions."

Some of the others grudgingly shared his amusement.

"Thanks to the protection of the Stars," began Lydan, "we are all still here to attend."

"Here, here!" cried the Dwarves and the Trolls.

"Thanks be to you, oh Great Stars," intoned the Faeries.

"Aye, we are all here," agreed Nevod. "But are we all well?"

"A very good question, sir." Witon nodded, pushing back the still wet plaits of his long white hair. "Let us take a moment and tell each other how we came through our disaster."

"Our arm muscles are sprained and swollen, I fear." Jwara sat quietly beside her husband. They rested their short, plump forearms, wrapped tightly in rags, tenderly upon their meager laps.

"We held fast to the main beam," Swerin reported, his long gray beard quivering. "That monster of an ocean would not get us."

"We thank the Stars you survived. Your company and talents would have been a great loss to us," Witon said sincerely.

"Uganta and Turatan wrapped our arms," Jwara offered timidly, saucer-shaped blue eyes looking to her left where the two young Trolls sat.

"Truly?" Witon asked.

"Truly," Jwara confirmed with a cheery nod.

To hear of care and cooperation between these creatures was as miraculous as their survival.

"We suffered only a few cuts," Uganta reported shyly, lowering his head covered with broad, wire-like black hair.

"It was our pleasure," said Turatan, with a nod to Jwara. His voice cracked with his youth.

Uganta nodded enthusiastically, a playful smile spreading across his perpetually snarling lips, displaying the brown, fang-like teeth not yet grown to full size.

"Once Flerial stitched us up, we were fine."

"She did a splendid job on many of us," piped up a tiny, lyrical voice.

Vishena sat regally on the back of the enormous Centaur Chiron, who stood at the back of the circle. Upon her lap, Flerial's bandaged head rested, tiny eyes closed, almost inaudible purring sounds of slumber floated up from her bud-like mouth.

"Is she all right, Your Highness?" Mitren asked, studying the Faerie's motionless form.

"She will be, as will I, dear man." Vishena rewarded him with her beautiful smile.

"How were you injured, dear?" Jwara asked Vishena with maternal concern, though she was years younger than the Faerie Queen.

"It's actually an amusing anecdote." Vishena's tiny hand stroked the blonde, almost white hair of the ethereal beauty in her lap.

"I'm not so sure of that, Your Majesty." Chiron's deep voice rumbled up with ill-concealed contrition. "We are so very sorry."

"Nonsense, pet. You and Chalene saved our lives," Vishena assured him tenderly, before turning back to face the Council eagerly awaiting her words with rapt curiosity, the crackling, spitting fire forgotten at their feet. "We were sitting upon their mighty backs when the storm hit.

When it struck, they captured us in their mighty hands and somehow managed to keep them closed throughout the entire ordeal."

"I'm afraid I held on a little too tightly," Chiron said gruffly, through a sheepish grin. "I did it, it was I who broke Vishena's wing."

"Tut, tut, dear one, no worries." Vishena shimmered at him and continued. "When Chalene hit the beach, she lost consciousness, dumping Flerial out. Her head struck a rock when she landed."

"To be injured by your savior is ironic indeed, Vishena, but we are grateful for your survival, whatever the means. Is she unconscious?" Witon gestured to the unmoving creature in Vishena's lap.

"No, no, her head is bruised but not seriously." Vishena looked down at the sleeping sprite, pride glowing in her eyes. "No, she is only exhausted. She spent every moment of every hour till this one, treating those who needed her."

"She worked miracles with my sister." Chiron stamped around the circle until he stood next to his sister. "Too tiny to treat Chalene herself, she hovered above her for hours, instructing others precisely how to do it. Her stamina, her knowledge, her patience..." he shook his head in awestruck admiration, "... they were truly amazing."

"My leg is broken," Chalene announced, before her brother could say any more and small gasps of dismay hissed like steam around the fire, drowning out the lugubrious pounding of the ocean waves in the distance. For a Centaur, there could be no more serious a wound than a broken leg; it would require months and months to heal. The inactivity it forced upon such a creature could be hazardous to the Centaur's general health.

"But my brother fares well," Chalene said with a hopeful lilt and a pale smile, dark eyes lighting on her restless brother. No one could mistake their familial bond; both were ruddy-skinned, dark-eyed and crowned with black, curly hair; Chiron's falling to his shoulders while his sister's reached her wide, equine back.

"True," Chiron agreed. "I have only small cuts and bruises and a couple of broken fingers on one hand." He flexed the bandaged appendage, as large as one of the small boulders in and around their meeting site.

"Flerial will see to it that I stay well," said Chalene, smiling at the still form of the Faerie. "I have no doubt."

"As she has already done for me," Nevod said, stroking his long bi-colored goatee. "Thirty-seven of her tiny little stitches now hold me together."

He held the large, bandaged arm up like one of his many medals.

"I almost passed out myself just watching her flying to and fro." The warrior Elf's golden green eyes sparkled with delight. He flung his muscular body back and forth in imitation, his long, corkscrew hair flaying about.

"You have never passed out in your life," Lydan said from the ground, looking up at his brother, eyes and mouth smiling fondly at him. "And considering that you're two hundred and sev—"

"Do... not... dare!" Nevod jumped up, wagging a long, thin, threatening finger in front of Lydan's long thin nose.

"—that you're as old as ye are, 'tis quite a feat," Lydan amended with a small chuckle, shifting his awkward position as he did so. Nevod saw his brother's discomfort and quickly took Lydan's shoulders, helping him to adjust until Lydan sat comfortably once more, his wrapped and slung right arm and splinted left leg making his easeful position a peculiar one.

"Anything else, brother?" Nevod asked, staring with deep concern into eyes so like his own.

"Nay, brother. 'Tis better, thank you," Lydan answered tenderly, and there in their words, the intangible but unbreakable bond between them became tangible.

"Are they broken?" Jwara asked of Lydan, pointing to his wounds. "I can make some ointment which will speed their healing."

"Nay, good lady, they are not broken, merely badly sprained. But I may make use of your potion still. I am sure I will be well in no time." He smiled at her gladly, injured, yet still luminescent with natural inner harmony. "As will we all, yes?"

Nevod stood once more, hands gesturing wide to the assemblage.

"Hear him, my brother, the diplomat. He will have us all convinced that we are on holiday soon."

Nevod's joke met with chuckles and smiles and not one twang of disbelief.

"I will take some of your ointment as well, good lady," Climora's small voice chimed in. "Both Brasher and I suffer bruised ribs from the ordeal. I believe such a tonic would help us much."

"How were you—?"

"I'll tell ye how we were hurt," Brasher cut Turatan off. "A crew member, though I'm not sure which, grabbed us, he did. Just as the storm burst upon us. Grabbed us and threw us in his pocket... his pocket!"

Brasher jumped up, hands on hips, his powerful but small arms bulging as one bare foot tapped impatiently on the top of the wide oak tree stump, indignation coursing through his small, sleek body.

"All that bouncing around. It's a wonder our heads are not broken!" Brasher's ire rose to full tempo. He brought one tightly fisted hand up, pounding the air with it as he spoke. "And if I find out which one it was, I will thrash him within an inch of his life."

Climora starred at him, one fuzzy eyebrow raised high upon her small forehead. "You mean you will thrash an inch of him?"

Nevod coughed loudly, a strange, clogged-throat bark, but he could not completely hide the upturn to the corners of his mouth; nor could others around the circle of flames.

"I will be sure to talk to the person responsible," Witon assured Brasher, feeling no need to share the fact that he would reward said person for saving the lives of the two Brownies!

"And you, brother?" Witon turned to Mitren, hoping to distract the Brownie from his simmering anger... anger that simmered often but never boiled over.

"I am well, Witon. I have rope and sand burns on most of my exposed skin, but that seems to be the extent of it." Mitren displayed the red and raw spots with a smirk and a shrug.

Witon silently thanked the Stars. He could not have borne the pain if harm or death had come to his brother. Unlike Witon, Mitren did not feel the need to change the world. He would, however, follow his brother to the ends of the universe, if Witon wished. At times, it was a heavy loyalty for him to bear.

"And you, dear Witon?" Vishena asked, a sultry smile upon her inquisitive face.

"Just my head," Witon said with a laugh.

Witon's only injury, ironically, was the one he took to the back of his head; the one he'd suffered in his cabin aboard the *Freedom*. Unbeknownst to him, he'd split his skull open, requiring many of Flerial's stitches to close it back up.

Witon gently rubbed the offending, still throbbing injury.

"Most of the crew survived. Only two hands perished, as you already know." Witon referred to the two burial services held earlier in the day.

They'd laid the bodies to rest in a small plot of field found just beyond the tree line. At this moment, two other crewmen were hard at the task of erecting a crude fence to protect and partition off the area, ground that Witon now considered hallowed.

"Do we know where we are?" asked Uganta.

"Do we know *when* we are?" Turatan blurted forcefully, but such bluster was no more than fear in disguise.

"From what we've deduced by the location of the constellations, 'tis two nights since the storm first struck," Vishena answered in her small, firm voice. Earlier in the day, she and Nevod had spent hours on these calculations.

"That means the storm lasted over a day and a half," Jwara mumbled, unblinking blue eyes locked upon the flames before her, words sparking from deep within muddied thoughts.

"As to where we are? We have not yet been able to answer." Witon turned to his brother.

"Once things settled down this morning," Mitren began, referring to those first few frantic hours of consciousness consumed with caring for the injured and the dead, "six of our best surveyors were sent to scout out the land. Two to walk the entire shoreline to ascertain the shape and circumference, two left for the north and east, and the other two traveled south and east. Without knowing how vast the land is, we have no clue as to when they'll return. Unfortunately, it may take days before they complete their mission."

The words hung heavily in the small circle and their import dampened not only the Council members' spirits but seemingly the fire itself; the flames dwindled to tiny wisps of pale yellow, their tips lost into the air and away, fading to sparks, then to nothing.

Climora shivered, her tiny teeth chattering loudly enough for the others to hear. Turatan got up, fetched more wood and swiftly placed it on the fire, the pungent, turpentine scent of burning pine bursting in the air.

"This place… wherever… whatever… it may be, it is not…" Uganta began, his large head swaying pensively as it hung below his wide shoulders.

"No, dear," Jwara said. "It isn't. It isn't like any place we have ever seen, is it?"

The question could be addressed to no one, or to all of them.

Sidelong, wary gazes slipped around the fire, from face to chary face.

Witon's breath hitched in his chest. There it was, out in the open. What he had been thinking, feeling, all day, as the nuances of this place revealed itself. The deed belonged to him, to bring it out of the shadows, but he would do it his way.

"It is one of the most beautiful places I have ever seen."

Every gaze fell upon him and in them, he saw their fear begin to scurry away.

"The plants and trees, they are so very much richer, more colorful."

"And strange," Brasher grunted.

"Yes, Brasher," Witon said with a smile, "and strange. But a wondrous strange."

"Wondrous," Vishena whispered, lips curling gently.

"And those fish," Mitren said, and his brother beside him could feel Mitren's shoulders gently rise and fall with his sigh. "Like nothing I've ever seen. But so much meatier."

"And tastier." Turatan licked his lips as if a smidgen of the delicious flavor lingered upon them.

Witon nodded, smiling broadly. "Yes, this place is strange, but in the most magnificent of ways. It is more... it is more..." He struggled to find the right word to describe this land and his feelings of it.

"It is just that... *more*," Swerin said for Witon.

Witon dropped his head back on his shoulders and looked up into a sky deeper than any he had ever seen, yet populated by more stars than he knew existed. He sunk into the absolute truth of Swerin's words. Leaning over, he squeezed the Dwarf's shoulder.

"Too right, good sir. It is so much more. And for that, I am grateful," Witon said.

The ayes came from them all, some still tinged with fear, fear of the unknown, but not without gratitude for the abundance and beauty which held them all prisoner.

"If we must be lost," Climora chirped, "being lost in paradise is not the worst place to be. We will most surely all grow fat until the scouts return."

"Indeed. There is everything we need... and more," Lydan said, with a wink to Swerin, an assurance only his brother recognized as slightly forced. "And with each passing minute, the crew is finding more and more of the ships' supplies where they've washed ashore."

Grunts and spirited nods gave agreement; all were amazed at how much of the vessel's stores were already on hand, everything from weapons—bows, arrows, and swords—to kitchen supplies and dishes that would, no doubt, go unused for many a day. At least ten crewmembers constantly scavenged up and down the shoreline, gathering items as they washed in on the tide's ebb and flow. The pile of materials grew so large that it quite hid Persky, centered in its midst, making an account of the ever-growing inventory.

In the hands of the irreplaceable Persky, Witon felt such precious commodities were quite safe.

The Council members looked to the growing heap of goods and for some, its ever-enlarging mass brought comfort, as did the sight of Persky himself. His very mixed blood served as a reminder for the homeland these creatures hoped to create.

"If we can just…" began Witon, but stopped, alerted by the sound of raised voices. He turned toward the clamoring and spied two crewmen rushing toward Persky with a large, dark, and oddly shaped object held between them. Persky took one glance at the item balanced in their cradled arms, spoke no more than a few gape-mouthed words, then thrust a commanding finger toward Witon.

Having watched the entire silent vignette, Witon stood to greet the men and the prophetic moment rushing toward him.

"My lord, my lord," one of the men shouted, "look what we've found!"

Out of breath, the heaving men stopped before the Council and lifted the large piece of wood before them like a shield.

The gasping trumped the crackling fire and rushing surf. In the shocked silence, Lydan brought his hands together, and then together again. Within seconds, the entire committee joined his applause. The ovation reached out over the sand, calling to the scattered crew. A quick glimpse at the found item, and they too cheered thunderously.

Jagged edges rimmed the haggard piece of wood; holes appeared where small pieces had disappeared, nabbed by the grasp of the storm. What lay upon the wood had survived the storm perfectly intact. What lay upon the wood in unspoiled composition were the golden letters spelling the word that both defined and feed them:

Freedom.

The happy eruption waned, leaving behind an altered assemblage, each creature's face changed; tired eyes glowed, pale cheeks bloomed with rosy color, and for the first time that day, smiles outnumbered frowns.

"Good friends!" Witon shouted, climbing up on one of the large rocks, long white hair flowing out behind him as the excited crowd stilled, their hopeful faces raised expectantly. "Good friends, I can think of no better time to call it a night. We have all suffered through this day. We have all worked hard, but now, with this sign of hope, let us rest. Let us take to our beds with hope in our hearts and the promise of the future on our minds."

The cheering crested once more and, as man and creature made their way to the bedrolls set out for them, Witon watched them shaking hands and patting each other on the back. He felt a hand come to rest on his own and turned to see who put it there.

Lydan's good hand rested genially on Witon's shoulder and a kind smile rested on his lips.

"You will get us safely through," Lydan said softly. "I have no doubt."

Witon nodded with silent gratitude. Nevod arrived at Lydan's side and helped him away to a bedroll. Witon stood alone, the power of hopeful spirits surrounding him in this circle. He took a step away and turned back, halted by the silhouette of a sitting Human form remaining near the Council meeting spot. The young woman, Katrin, worked furiously on the parchment balanced on her knees.

Belamay.

Seeing the artist, brought her quickly into his mind. Just the thought of her, his soul mate, sent shivers of delight coursing through him. He needed her unwavering, unconditional love more than ever, needed to remember it, to hold tight to it.

"You will harm your eyes working in this dim light," he said to Katrin, approaching the artist through the gloom.

She turned with a startled flinch, revealing an unbecoming patch upon her freckled face.

"Well, your eye, rather."

His jest elicited naught more than a dead-pan gaze from Katrin's one uncovered eye, sliding away as the artist resumed her work.

"I'm just about done," she said and, with a few flourishing strokes, held up the drawing.

The small grin on Witon's face grew to a magnificent smile. Upon the page lay an uncanny rendering of the very first meeting of the Council of Creatures. The depth and talent of her strokes brought each creature to vivid life. Witon squinted in the growing gloom and looked closer to see the smallest details.

Katrin saw his study and frowned.

"If ye wish," she said, eyes jumping from her work to his face, "I can fix it."

"Nay," Witon said quietly, still smiling. "Leave us just as you have us."

Katrin brought the rendering back to her knees and smiled at her own work. There they were, a group unlike any her world had ever known. They each wore their bandages and splints, dressings and supports as proudly as they would any medal or commendation. But they sported something else as well, every one of them. They all wore the same look, from the smallest to the largest; they all wore the look of hope.

Chapter XIV

UNKNOWN WORLDS APART

Could such a short time bring so much misery?

How then, thought Belamay, *did the birds dare sing?*

Donning her favorite riding habit, leather and linen with a touch of lace, worn so often it felt like a second skin, Belamay needed the rush of speed to speed time; needed the challenge of forming one being with a charging animal to relieve her of tension. Witon departed but three days ago and yet his absence stabbed like a wound she could not heal, a hole she could not fill.

They should arrive today; today is the day. The mantra refused to leave her mind. It blotted out other thoughts as the storm clouds gathering in the sky did the sun, which her preoccupied mind failed to see.

"Not too long a ride, m'lady," the young Josem dared to advise, as his cupped hands helped Belamay up and astride the saddle pad and her favorite destrier, his deep loyalty and affection for his mistress overriding decorum. "Looks like a storm will soon be upon us."

She peered up then; how low the clouds hovered above her, how widely they cast their gray gloom. But thoughts of storms only added to her vexation and she picked up the reins, eager to snap them, keen for her and Starfire to be off, to run from their pestering.

"No fear, Josem," Belamay said with a half-hearted smile, "just a short jaunt to the shore and back, no more."

"Very well, m'lady, but—"

His words came too late. With a stinging *whap* of the leather in her hands and a harsh "Hi-yah!" she set off.

She did not ease her horse to a trot, no gradual build-up to speed, but a sudden burst of it instead.

Belamay lifted herself on her stirrups and hunkered her shoulders down low. It took no more than minutes to have the worrisome mantra plaguing her since Witon's departure replaced with the rhythmic *thubalup, thubalup* of Starfire's galloping hooves.

The forest closed in around her, the path a thin strip amidst tightly woven trees, a ribbon of brown, packed earth through prickly deep green leaves and the ferns carpeting the ground beneath them. The briny scent of the sea beckoned as she raced toward it. But still, she needed more speed.

Belamay tapped her heels to her horse's flanks; the chanting came faster... *thubalup, thubalup, thubalup*; she squatted ever farther down, closer and closer to her steed's own shoulders, his bobbing head. She could barely see above them for she trusted this dear beast, as she felt them move as one. So intent on the moment, the motion... so in tune and trusting in her steed, it rendered her blind to all else.

In that moment of bliss, the men burst out from the thick foliage.

Belamay hung on as her horse reared. Suddenly, she saw nothing save looming sky as her body lurched backward. Screeching pierced the air, the scream of her horse in fright. Together, they roiled up and over. Together, they crashed toward the ground.

Belamay hit first, flat on her back, her breath rushing from her painfully, her head snapping on her neck. In a flash of time, all she would have, Belamay knew she had to move, had to roll, before her horse followed her to the earth.

With a hideous gasp for air, she lifted her left shoulder and dug her right into the ground, twisting her body.

She wasn't quick enough; Starfire found her. As his long, heavy torso slammed to the ground, her left leg caught between the two colliding forces of earth and horse.

Belamay screamed in pain, flashes of light bursting in her eyes though they had squeezed shut with the searing agony.

Starfire scrambled in the ungainly way horses regain their footing, and Belamay released a strangled cry... relief from the weight upon her limb, relief that he remained unharmed.

She opened her eyes; her heart missed beats uncounted.

The man's face hovered no more than inches from hers. His yellow, jagged teeth and fetid breath curled her lip with disgust.

"Have no fear, m'lady." He grinned hideously at her. "We'll take good care of ye, won't we, lads?"

Belamay opened her eyes fully. As the flashes of light burst once more in her gaze, she saw armed men, glittering swords, pin-sharp daggers. She tried to sit up, to run, to fight, but her head swam and he pushed her down.

"Oh no, missus. You go nowhere but with us."

As he and another grabbed her by the shoulders, fingers digging into muscular flesh, Belamay's head fell back between them. She heard and saw no more.

* * *

He made quite the strangest picture, perched at the fancy desk, studiously poring over the parchments covering its salt-powdered surface. He belonged in an opulent library, surrounded by leather-bound books and great art, not atop a sand dune with the lapping waves of a high tide gurgling nearby.

Witon's desk had survived the storm and the wreck in one piece, washing up on the shore near camp. His heart had fluttered with pleasure when he saw the small but impressively carved piece of mahogany. It felt as if his mother had found him here, wherever 'here' was.

As soon as he found it, he had set it up on its feet, there on the high mound of sand and worked diligently from it a few hours every day. His fellow survivors laughed to see him sitting there, the ocean's waves threatening to pull him and the wood back into its clutches, a gentleman at work in the strangest sort of study. And yet, seeing Witon hard at work had a soothing effect on those around him, allaying fears, making it feel as if there was something right with this world.

From his strange post on the shore, Witon conferred over the list of stores with Persky, the updated condition of the injured with Glasion, the Medical Advisor and, as he did at this moment, he made entries in his Captain's log. The original log had survived within its locked desk drawer, though its pages were now bumpy, curled, and yellow after drying out in the sun.

Captain's Log, Witon wrote, *Third day of the First Spring Moon in the year Fourteen Hundred Twelve.*

It has been eight days since the storm washed us up on these shores, eight days and not a single scouting party has returned. I begin to fear for their safety.

Those of us in camp are faring well, regardless of our situation. There is abundant game and fish to feed us and we have erected lean-tos for shelter in case of rain, though none has been encountered since the storm. Everyone's injuries are healing nicely. Chalene's was by far the worst but Flerial and Glasion watch her closely.

My own hard head is almost completely healed, but the pain inside it grows every day, the pain of waiting.

Witon placed the feather he'd fashioned into a quill gently on the desktop and flexed the clenched fingers of his writing hand, though it was not only from scripting that his hand throbbed. Like the others, Witon rarely needed to search for things to do; he hunted and fished, searched the shore for items that continued to wash ashore daily, and helped erect the shelters from pieces of wood and fragments of *Freedom's* large sails. Yet too much free time plagued him, empty hours allowing fear to creep into his thoughts. When it did, he would stand at the water's edge and gaze first in one direction and then the other, hoping and praying—willing the scouts to return. Hours passed as he flipped his head back and forth, staring at naught but emptiness for miles on either side.

Witon tipped his head this way and that, stretching tight neck muscles as he scanned the skies above. He would write no more tonight; the sun's light waned and his head throbbed from the strain of seeing in the dark. Witon put paper, quill, and ink into the shallow top drawer of the desk and rose, his feet instantly chilling in the cold beach sand as he strode to the shelters where others already slept. He took to his bedroll and lay upon it, but found sleep elusive despite his exhaustion.

Like most nights, he tossed and turned, trying to form the sand below him to fit his body comfortably while he played the "what ifs" over and over in his mind. Witon thought he slept for a time, but it felt like the briefest of moments, a sleep devoid of dreams and rejuvenation, when someone rudely jostled him awake.

Witon cracked open one eye and looked up, but he saw only blackness.

"Either I am blind or whoever dares wake me cannot discern night from day."

"I'm so sorry, Milord," Persky whispered.

Perched on his knees, the young Elf man leaned close to his Captain's face, not wishing to disturb others nearby. "But I really think you'll want to wake up. One of the scouting parties has returned."

Witon flung himself upwards, his head conking Persky's with a crack.

"Good Stars!" they exclaimed, laughing together through their pain at the comedy of their inelegance.

"Are ye all right, Persky?" Witon whispered, not waiting for an answer. "Where are they?"

Rubbing his forehead, where a large lump already formed at the point of impact, Persky pointed to the two men sitting by the main fire.

Witon ran, crossing the beach with a few large, furious strides. Recognizing Igar and Elson, two of his long-standing crew members, he embraced them both, relieved just to see them alive. With flapping hands, he motioned for them to sit back down, asked Persky, now recovered enough to join them, to get them some food, and sat down with them.

"You traveled southeast, correct?" Witon questioned and the two men nodded their heads as they stuffed pieces of the smoked meat Persky brought them into their mouths.

"Tell me everything."

Igar, the older and a more experienced explorer, hesitated. The deepness of the night, the profoundness and the quietness, overwhelmed him as every man, creature, beast, and bird around them slept. Elson, younger and more muscular, encouraged Igar to recount their adventures with a thrust of his square jaw.

"We've never seen a land like this, m'Lord," Igar began, a fitting start to a tale of creatures unnamable, of forests of such majesty they were nature's cathedral, of rivers so alive, one could not tell where the water ended and the life within began.

"He asked me over and over," Elson piped in, "are we dead and among the Great Stars? Is this is what life is like among them?"

Igar pushed his travel mate's shoulder, but playfully so, and they both smiled with wonder.

Witon caught the contagion of it, and smiled as well.

"I took the liberty of attempting to chart the ground we covered," Igar said, pulling a crumpled piece of foolscap out of his rucksack. "I'm not much of an artist but I think it gives a good representation of the land we covered."

Witon grabbed the paper from Igar's hand, too excited for polite restraint. He squatted down close to the fire. After but a few moments, he looked up at Igar, with confusion, not pleasure, twisting his comely features.

"Are you sure this is accurate?"

"Aye, My Lord. As I said, the drawings aren't pretty but they're precise."

Witon stood, holding the map in one hand and with the other, gestured for them to stop.

"Wait, wait!" He tore across the beach as if chased by an invisible force. Igar and Elson shared a raised brow look of confusion.

"Wait for what?" Igar whispered to Elson, but Elson merely shrugged his shoulder and stuffed more food in his mouth.

They didn't have long to wonder. Within moments, Witon returned with a piece of paper of his own and thrust it into Igar's hand.

"Look at this and tell me what ye think."

Igar took Witon's paper close to the fire. He looked up at Witon, bushy salt and pepper brows knitting together, jaw slacking and dropping.

"Could it be?"

"It certainly looks like it, does it not?" Witon tried very hard not to smile, knowing he needed more information, for the other scouting parties to return, but the amazing possibility almost defied belief. "Say nothing to anyone. I would not want to give false hope to so many who need true faith, until we know for sure."

"Of course, My Lord," said Igar, "but if this is true...?"

"I know, my good man." Witon clapped his hand warmly on Igar's shoulder. "'Twould truly be a miracle from the Stars."

* * *

"This cannot be happening," he groaned, rolling over in his makeshift bed and looking up through one squinted eye. He saw nothing but blackness. "Persky? Is that you?"

"Aye, My Lord."

Witon flew up to a sitting position. Persky, prepared this time, sat well back from Witon, out of harm's way.

"More have arrived?"

"Aye, My Lord."

"Where?"

"By the fire, sir."

Witon jumped up and ran off, kicking sand up into Persky's face, getting it in Persky's mouth and eyes.

"I certainly hope the next group arrives during the day," Persky muttered to himself between cleansing spits. "If not, I am waking his lordship with a very long stick."

Witon reached the two men sitting by the fire and embraced them, delighting in their survival. This time, however, he wasted very little breath on small talk.

"Did ye by any chance chart a map of the areas you traveled? You voyaged north-east, correct?"

"Aye, My Lord, on both counts," said Yerten, a middle-aged man with intelligent eyes and a friendly face. He reached into his pack on the ground in front of him, bringing out a creased, scarred paper. "I am trained in surveying. I have it right—"

Witon couldn't wait. He grabbed the foolscap from Yerten's hand and once again squatted by the fire.

"Oh… my… Stars," Witon stuttered. He stood up and, with a blazing smile on his face, pinched Yerten's cheek.

"Wait right here, do not move," Witon ordered excitedly and strode away, foolscap in hand.

Yerten rubbed his pinched cheek.

"What the Stars was that?" he asked his companion, Orkley by name, a man the same age as Yerten but taller and broader.

Orkley shook his head and laughed around the large pieces of food in his mouth.

"Methinks he likes ye."

Yerten coshed his friend smartly on the back of his head.

"Don't be disrespectful. The man's been under a lot of pressure lately, do ye not think?"

Orkley didn't get the opportunity to respond, as Witon returned, another man in tow, a man smiling as broadly as Witon.

"This is the map Igar here has made." Witon gave the paper to Yerten as Igar and Yerten exchanged nods of greeting. "And this is another map I'd like ye to look at."

Yerten studied the three papers then looked up at Witon and Igar. He stared at them intently for another moment. He took a deep, steadying breath through his nose, inhaling the tangy scent of damp, burning timber. He returned to his perusal of the papers. He put his and Igar's maps together and held them in one hand, while in his other he held Witon's. The man's absorption with the diagrams went on for some minutes, but Witon didn't stand and wait for his conclusion. He turned his face to the shore and watched as the brilliant stars began to dim in readiness for the coming dawn.

"Amazing," Yerten said, but seemed unable to say any more.

"Truly," Witon answered, turning back to the men. "I'm starting to feel, starting to hope it could be true, but again I ask you, Igar, and now you, Yerten, not to say aught to anyone until we know for sure."

"Of course, My Lord," answered both men.

"I wouldn't want to get their hopes up prematurely," Witon explained to Yerten.

"Too late for me, sir," Yerten muttered.

* * *

He expected it. He waited for it. Witon lay awake in his bedroll. Tonight, he waited for them. Two nights in a row, Persky had woken him up with news of returning scouting parties. The news these men had brought filled Witon with such hope, his heart felt ready to burst from his chest. All day, as he went about his usual chores, he heard it beating in his ears. He came to think of it as an internal clock ticking away the time until the next and last scouting party returned.

He knew he wore a silly grin upon his face. He saw it reflected in the bewildered gaze of those who looked at him askance all day, but he couldn't help himself. If it were true, if such a monumental miracle had been gifted to them, it was both mystifying and miraculous.

If... he thought and rolled over in his bedroll with a groan.

Witon searched the sky for his favorite constellation and wondered if Belamay lay in her bed, looking out her window at the same stars. He saw her there, in her thin, white lace and linen gown, her hair flowing like petals around her smiling face. He inhaled the lavender scent that always seemed to surround her, could almost feel the silk-like softness of her skin.

Witon groaned again, this time jumping up out of his sleeping roll in surrender. Such thoughts would just make the night unbearably longer. He looked about and saw all the bodies peaceful in slumber. He looked to the four compass points and saw the night guards diligently manning their posts. He knew not how long he had lain there counting stars but when first he went to bed, the tide tumbled in at its highest. Now the fecund, fecal smell of a very low tide assaulted his nostrils. He needed to get away from it.

Witon walked to the tree line and inhaled the wonderful pine scent, flushing his nostrils of the offending odor. He turned and began walking northward, allowing his mind to wander and relax, enjoying the beauty surrounding him.

Were these trees pine? If so, they were by far the biggest he had ever seen, their needles longer and brighter, their scent sharper. Such thoughts he let meander in and out.

He had no idea how far he walked, or for how long. Before he knew it, the edges of the sky to his right flushed with day's first light. Low clouds hung on the horizon's edge, their flat bases growing brighter, and their tops darker and more visible. The seagulls began their morning cries of greeting as they scavenged for food along the tide line, which rose higher now, mercifully producing a less offensive aroma.

He headed toward the shoreline, then back in the direction he'd come. He stopped for a moment, surprised at how far he'd traveled; he couldn't see camp, no matter how far he peered into the distance.

Witon shrugged and began the leisurely walk back. Time passed; the quietness consumed him. He found peace in the feel of cool sand between his toes and with the plover-like, little feathered creatures that chased him up the shoreline.

In the near distance, he watched a flock of birds trying to take flight, only to be pulled back to earth. He continued at a leisurely pace, counting pearly white rocks to keep his mind clear. Glancing ahead, he saw the same movement. He squinted at it… this was no flock of feathered phantoms. It was a small group of men, his men, jumping up and down, waving their arms excitedly. His steps faltered.

"Great Stars, not now!"

He started running. He ran past crabs and snails making their tedious way on shore. He ran as seagulls screeched at him for disturbing their breakfast table. He ran and ran until he felt as if his lungs failed him and his legs could no longer move.

Witon crashed to a stop at Persky's feet and those of two other men.

Persky looked down at his master lying prostrate on the shore, wheezing for breath and rubbing his legs.

"They're here, My Lord."

Witon nodded, his breathing still so strained he had no air to talk. He reached for one of the men and took his hand. That man, Miltra, thought Witon required help getting up; instead, he found himself pulled down onto the beach next to Witon and clasped in a crushing embrace.

"You've... returned," Witon got out, his sporadic breathing disturbing his speech. "Thank... the... Stars, you've returned."

"Uh... yes, My Lord, we have," Miltra said and pulled himself from the embarrassing embrace, standing up as quickly as possible. He motioned to his brother, Lusby, and the two men bent down and pulled Witon onto his feet.

Witon pushed his long, sand-infested hair from his eyes and stared at the two men he'd waited for so anxiously, his expression swiftly changing to one of stark surprise. He pointed to them, first one, then the other, then the first yet again.

"Did you... uh... did you look like... *that*... when you left?"

For all Witon's urgency to know what these two men had encountered and to see a map—if any—that they'd produced, their physical appearance so startled him that for a moment he forgot aught else.

Tall and young, with incredible blue eyes, they both possessed the lightest, almost white blond hair he'd ever seen. Even their eyebrows looked like two white slashes above their eyes.

Miltra and Lusby burst out laughing. This was not the first time they'd heard such a question, but Witon's incredulity was writ comically upon his fine features.

"Aye, My Lord," Lusby chuckled. "We're explorers by trade. Some have nicknamed us the Ghosts."

Witon nodded. "Of course." He had heard of these men. He had asked his brother to retain them as part of the crew because of their reputation, though he had thought their moniker referred to their stealth, not their appearance.

"I think you're anxious to see this, sir." Miltra handed Witon a piece of paper. Persky had obviously hinted at the Count's curiosity.

Witon took the paper and for a moment—a mere sliver of time—he hesitated, anxious doubt holding him firm. He shook off his fear and gazed down at the paper. One good look and he knew.

"Yes!" He fairly screamed the words. "Oh, Good Stars, yes!"

He jumped about as if his feet were on fire. He grabbed Miltra and Lusby and hugged them, forcing them to jump up and down with him. He grabbed Persky, lifted him up and threw him back down, making the poor fellow land roughly on his backside. With one adrenaline-fired hand, Witon reached down and pulled Persky back up, kissing him smartly on his cheek.

"'Tis true, Persky, 'tis true."

Chapter XV

REVELATIONS

Witon ran, sprinting for camp. He stopped short, sand flying up about his feet, and looked at the three stunned creatures behind him.

"Well, come on. We have to tell them," Witon ordered and the other three ran to catch up.

* * *

This, the Council of Creatures' second meeting, donned a different cloak than the first. This time, the news shone as bright as the orange sun in the cloudless violet sky. They shared fish stew and a cup of ale as they spoke their thoughts about the miraculous occurrence.

"You are quite right, Witon," Vishena said from her perch on his shoulder. "'Tis truly a miracle. The Stars may have put a terrible storm in our path, but they have guided us to our destination, our home, nonetheless."

The joy had spread throughout the entire camp as Witon told the Council, and Persky told the crew: they had, in actual fact, washed ashore on the very land to which they'd set their course. The Council heard the crew celebrating, strains of joyful music and voices loud with jubilation as cups clanged together in cheers.

"A marvel, yes, indeed. Almost beyond reckoning," said Chiron. "But the real problem is yet to be faced."

Through all his ruminations, as he waited for the scouting parties to return, Witon had refused to let his thoughts trip over the next hurdle. He knew it would have to be faced sooner or later, yet he needed to feel the thrill of one victory before engaging in the next battle.

"How do we let the others on Minra Enra know we are here?" Swerin spoke it aloud, the challenge not so easily conquered. "The original plan called for us to send the *Freedom* back for them. When it does not arrive as planned, they will surely think us lost."

"Could we build a small boat out of the *Freedom's* remains and send a few crew members back?" Uganta asked hopefully.

"It's a good thought," Mitren said quietly, scratching at the cloak worn by the bearer of bad news. "But I do not believe there is enough material left to erect a craft worthy of such a voyage. Not even the heartiest crewmembers could row such a distance. Besides, most of the navigational devices have been damaged beyond repair."

The Council grew quiet. To realize they had arrived upon the shores of their new world, only to be stranded here—alone, perhaps forever—brought them swiftly down from joyous heights to hard ground.

"I've been thinking of another way." Nevod shifted upon his rock chair, an uncharacteristic note of indecisiveness in his voice.

"By all means, let's hear it," Witon encouraged.

Nevod spared a glance at Lydan, sharing his brother's thoughts and encouragement.

"This may be hard for some to understand and believe," Lydan gave voice to his brother's idea. "We have learned, as have all Elves, to overcome the bonds of physical existence." Lydan smiled a crooked grin; such notions were often met with incomprehension from those of other species. "We are aware of the many myths about our race and our magical abilities, and whilst some are rightly not to be believed, others are. We do possess the capacity to communicate with our minds."

The Trolls and the Dwarves looked at each other skeptically but other members of the Council showed no reaction.

"I hold no doubts about your populace or their powers, Lydan," Witon responded. "Though I must admit, I did not know this… communication… was one of them."

"It is, sir," said Lydan, "but you must understand, 'tis not communication as you know it. We do not actually 'speak' to another."

"Then how does it work?" Turatan asked, genuine curiosity belying his gruff voice and gnarled expression.

Lydan leaned forward, resting the elbows of his long arms upon his leather-covered knees. "We are able to project our thoughts into the mind of another. The pictures we see in our minds are then pictured by the one we concentrate on."

"It seems difficult," Jwara said tenderly, her light eyes resting softly on Lydan's comely face.

"I would not say 'difficult'…" Lydan shrugged, while his brother shook his head, handsome face scrunched. "But it does require a great deal of concentration and, unfortunately, time."

"I get the most dreadful pain in my head," a small voice chirped and all eyes turned to Vishena in surprise.

"We, too… well, a few of us… have the same capability, of a type," she clarified, with not an iota of self-aggrandizement.

Witon sat back against the rock behind him and held out his palm for the Faerie Queen.

"Well," he said, smiling at the wee form glowing in his hand. "Thou art full of surprises, aren't you?"

Vishena's glow turned from white to pink and she smiled shyly at Witon.

"A lady must always keep some secrets, My Lord."

Lydan laughed with the others. "The most important aspect," he went on to explain, "is that we must decide clearly the images we wish to convey."

"Quite true," Vishena agreed.

"Ah, yes, understood." Witon rubbed his forehead in thought. "We don't want to alarm them, but they do need to know the *Freedom* will not be coming back for them."

Climora waved from her perch on the stump, eager to be heard. "They also need to know we have arrived at our ultimate destination."

"Too true," Mitren agreed. "They will need to follow the map and coordinates we used, as they will not have our ship to guide them."

"And more supplies," Brasher barked. "More ale."

"And make their way to us with the speed of the Great Stars," Jwara offered.

"We are here, follow original coordinates, more supplies, please come," Lydan said, consolidating the suggestions of the Council. "Does that seem right?"

"Exactly. And whomever you are able to reach should get in touch with Belamay. She knows how to reach all the others and together, they will find their way." Witon smiled, releasing a long, slow breath. A plan now existed, no matter how tenuous its success may appear. "Is there anything you need?"

"Peace and quiet is all I require. And you, Lydan?" asked Vishena.

"The same."

"Then will you start immediately?" Witon rose to his feet with their nodded agreements. "A year ago, I would not have believed this quest of mine, this idea of freedom, would ever happen. Now look at us. All together, creature with creature, on the land of our dreams, and it is more than any of us had ever imagined it. I have no doubt ye will be successful."

Witon's encouraging words lightened everyone's spirits, not just Lydan's and Vishena's.

"The waiting will be excruciating," said Chalene, stamping her large feet in the sand.

"The sitting about will make it worse," said Brasher from his tree stump perch.

"Then I suggest we keep ourselves busy." Nevod stood and opened outstretched arms, embracing their new home. "This is our land of freedom, is it not? Where we, and generations of our families to come, will make their homes?"

The Council concurred with a raucous chorus of nods and grunts.

"Then let's begin to build it."

"Aye," cheered the quiet Flerial, taking flight to flutter about Nevod's head. "Let's."

Witon's breath hitched; relief and excitement fluttered in his chest. He'd been thinking, wanting to do exactly as Nevod now suggested, but feared some may not be up for the task, being too stagnant in the fear-filled no place in which they existed.

"Wonderful." He clapped his hands together with enthusiasm. "I believe the first task is to decide where the center of government, where the Council, should be located."

He brought out his map, now thin and worn at the creases, and placed it on a flat rock.

"I believe this location would be the best." He pointed to an area of land surrounded by water, the ocean on one side, a forked river around the rest. "Not only does the water create a natural moat providing fortification, the location provides easy access to both drinking water and the natural harbors that lie on each side of the land. Plus, 'tis but a few miles from our present position, making the transfer of our camp an easy one."

The other Council members took turns to study the map. With a hearty chorus, all agreed Witon's plan made the most sense.

"I have no doubt a wondrous castle will one day exist there." Lydan expressed everyone's pleasure and hopes for the new kingdom they were creating.

"If we use all the wood of the *Freedom* to create large litters," Mitren suggested, "we can use them to carry other supplies to the site. Once we're all there, we can use them as walls, or at least the beginning of walls."

"And once we are there," Witon said to the group, but his eyes were focused much farther away, into the amazing future he saw for this land, "the real work will begin."

"I, for one, welcome such work with open arms," said Swerin, removing his red cap from his head and twisting it in his hands. "In my mind, I see the beautiful things I will create once my forge has arrived. I see stoves and watering devices; I see containers and farming equipment."

Swerin's words sent imaginations and dreams soaring and they all began to talk at once of their new kingdom and their visions for its future.

Witon wanted nothing more than to sit and dream with them, but he knew these dreams would only come true with hard work.

"Then let us begin," he said and spurred the others into action. As Centaur and Faerie, Brownie and Troll, Human and Dwarf stood and set off to join the crew, Lydan and Vishena stayed in their place. Witon almost laughed as he watched Uganta and Turatan stride away. They were so thrilled by the dreams of a new world, their abounding energy, not unlike that of any other young male, displayed itself in the jaunt of their step and the swing of their hairy arms.

"I will remain here," said Lydan. "I can think of nowhere better to try. The power of the hopeful spirits here will feed my abilities."

"Of course, stay right where you are," Witon concurred. "And you, Vishena dear?"

"I will fly," she answered, launching herself from his palm, wings beating so quickly they were but a blur of color behind her. "When I fly, my body is but a vessel for my mind."

With that, she launched into the sky and away.

Witon's eyes stayed on the brilliant point in the firmament until he lost sight of her.

"May the power of the Great Stars be with you both."

* * *

Slowly, the sounds of the Council and the crew dimmed, then disappeared altogether. Lydan sat crossed-legged upon the sand with his face to the ocean and the warm afternoon sun. The trees behind him swayed and rustled in the wind as the scent of cooking food, raw wood, and the sea's brine filled his nostrils. Lydan found stillness in his breath, releasing his being from his physical form. His brow furrowed and slowly, the color of fresh cream spread across his mind, cream and gold, softness and light.

There ye are, my dear, my love. 'Tis been so long since I've held you close, dear wife, but your beauty is always with me. I see your golden hair flying out behind you as you frolic in the woods of our dell. I see your eyes as they glow in the delight of the day. I see what you see, the dell alive with the spring day, the birds in flight, the butterflies and bees hovering from one blossom to another. But now you must see what I see. You must be here with me, with my spirit.

He saw Zelia stop her play. He saw her turn her head to the sun and the Stars hiding behind its brightness and knew she came to him, that they had joined, spiritually and mentally. Time passed uncounted as he existed in the two planes. The pictures rose up in his mind with the smallest effort. First, he saw the *Freedom* in pieces on the shore and then the Council and the surviving crew members. He visualized Witon's map, the one showing the land they'd all dreamed about. There stood Belamay, smiling, as she always seemed to be, opening the door he willed Zelia to knock upon. Lydan brought these two spiritual representations to the shipyard and helped them discuss the voyage with the captain. With a final push of empathic effort, he watched as the new vessel and its trekkers of creatures launched itself to him and their new world. Zelia stood on the bow and, as the vessel began its journey, she turned to the eye of Lydan's mind and blew him a kiss. With this mental picture, Lydan's spiritual connection ceased and he slumped onto the sand, exhausted.

He heard the sounds of this earthly reality first; people talking, crude spoons tinkling against dented plate. He opened one eye and saw a moonless sky, the darkness alive with stars.

"'Tis good, brother?"

Lydan turned to the voice and found Nevod, eating his evening meal as he sat on the ground next to Lydan.

"'Tis very good," Lydan answered with a smile. He sat up, took the plate of food from his brother's hands, and began devouring the remaining food.

Nevod leaned over, planted a kiss on his brother's forehead, and set off for another trencher of food.

* * *

The beauty of the land passed in a blur of color beneath her wings and, for a time, Vishena could only gaze down upon it in astonishment. The forests and glens, the river and all its springs, the fields of green and gold were breathtaking to behold. The vast landscape painted a picture of peace and prosperity.

I must get them here.

With such a thought, she began her attempts to reach Ventross, her younger brother who served as Regent in her absence.

Unlike Lydan, Vishena's thoughts were more encapsulated; broken boat, their new land, Belamay, navigation—bursting from her like a frenetic signal light. She visualized the images over and over until, as she said it would, the headache began. The first pangs of pain pinched at the edges of her mind, sending her back.

She returned to camp unnoticed, blending with the surroundings like a butterfly in a field of lilacs, until she landed on Witon's shoulder.

Coughing and spluttering, Witon choked on the piece of fish in his mouth, almost swatting Vishena from his shoulder as he would an offending insect.

"Welcome back, my dear." He swallowed the lump of food caught in his throat. "How are things?"

"Things are progressing," she replied with a yawn. She fluttered her wings and moved to a flat gray rock beside Witon. Flerial noted her Queen's return and brought her a small leaf heavy with food.

"And you?" Vishena asked the man beside her between tiny nibbles. "How are things?"

Witon had quit his seat upon the rock and now sat on the sand, his back resting on the granite upon which she sat, his head at the same level as the Faerie Queen's.

"Things are progressing wonderfully," Witon said, eager to update Vishena on the achievements the others had made.

The biggest pieces of wood were fashioned into large carts, ten in all. Tomorrow, they would begin to distribute all the goods and supplies evenly onto the litters, ensuring the weight was uniformly dispersed.

"Once that is done, we will begin the journey home." Witon's smile shone brilliantly white against his sun-exposed skin.

"Home..." Vishena breathed the word with the hush of a prayer.

Chapter XVI

SEEING TOO MUCH; SEEING ENOUGH

The stinging slap brought her back, brought her out of the darkness she had fallen into, with a harsh gasp. Belamay lifted her head, opened her eyes, but saw little more than shadows. She tried to move.

Then the pain hit her, in her arms and legs. She tried to move again, differently, and cried out with the agony of it. Ropes bound her, and tightly so. Though she stood, her captured arms were suspended above her head, bound to walls by chains. Her legs, spread and quivering, were ensnared in the same fashion. Her body formed a star of imprisonment. Any move, even the littlest sort, carried with it great pain, but no chance for escape.

"Ah, you are awake, finally." The snide, slippery male voice came at her from out of the shadows and Belamay blinked against the light of a torch suddenly lit, held between her and her captive. She could not see him at all.

"You have kept me waiting for some time."

She heard steps; steps upon stone, the scratch of dust between boot-heel and floor, a small rumble of laughter, other voices. They were not alone.

"And I don't like to be kept waiting."

From out of the darkness the hand flew, delivering a hard, brutal wallop as the back of it collided with her cheek, bringing tears to her eyes.

* * *

Vishena's eyes burst open in the dark. The tiny gaze flit all about. The stars still shone bright, though the waxing lavender moon vied for dominance in the night sky. She held her hand up to her face. Her left cheek burned, but why, she did not know.

She came more awake. And the fear found her.

Something was wrong, very wrong. Without a sound, she took flight; her mind must do its searching.

* * *

Belamay's head whipped back and dropped forward, onto her chest once more. Grinding her teeth, she brought it up. Even as the prick of pain spread across her jaw, she knew her captive stood close by now; he had to, in order to strike her so. She tasted the bitterness of blood as it trickled into her mouth.

She lifted her head and opened her eyes. Her stomach knotted and her innards cramped at what she saw.

A Lapith stood before her. A man, yes, but as tall and broad as a Centaur, with hard features and long hair. This man stared down at her, his heavy, almost cliff-like brow keeping his thin eyes in shadow. Though she had acquaintances among the species, Belamay knew him not.

"Wha..." she swallowed on a throat dry and parched, "...what do you want?"

"I have asked you twice already, do you not remember?"

Belamay shook her head, immediately wishing she hadn't. The pain screeched through her. A flash of memories returned... other moments just like this. The dizziness threatened to overtake her again.

* * *

Vishena's small body spun to the Earth; a whirling, out-of-control dive from which she could not recover. Her head swam with a blaze of wooziness. She hit the ground hard, thick grass softening the blow, her small body bouncing on it as she grunted.

Hidden amongst the tall blades of bright green, she sat up, one word in her mind, on her tongue...

"Lapiths."

* * *

"You know where they are. All your pain, your discomfort will end, when you tell us where." The Lapith paced around her, coming to stand close behind, so close his warm, fetid breath puffed hotly on her neck. Belamay shivered against the moist cling of it.

They wanted Witon—or rather, the Centaurs with Witon—and the destination, the location of the new world the Centaur nation planned to inhabit, an evolution of civilization she would gladly give her life for.

Holding as steady as she could, Belamay sniffed a spite-filled laugh. "I will tell you nothing. I will die first."

"Ah, we have a martyr here, my friends," the Lapith said and his sarcasm brought more low-toned snickering.

Belamay felt him lean closer still, his head—twice the size of her own—bent now next to her ear. Bile rose in her throat as hands the size of large rocks grabbed the back of her legs roughly. Too slowly they moved, rubbing up till they grabbed her buttocks and squeezed, hard.

"You are willing to die for your cause. How very touching." He spoke in her ear and the hate in his voice echoed in her pounding head. "But there are things much worse than death."

His hand shot between her legs, foot-long fingers digging into tender flesh, and she screamed with the pain.

* * *

Lydan bolted awake, the scream on his lips.

"What? Who?" Nevod rolled on the ground beside him, grabbing his sword and jumping up at the same time. Holding the blade before him, he crouched in a posture of defense.

"No, oh no."

Nevod peered down at his brother. He sat rod-straight, rocking slightly to and fro, seemingly awake. And yet his eyes were squeezed tightly closed.

Nevod dropped to his knees before him.

"What is it, brother? What do you see?"

Lydan's lids flew open. His tender green eyes screamed with fear; his voice, when it came, cracked upon the single word, "Belamay."

* * *

Belamay closed her eyes against the pain, struggling against the chains that bound her, longing to fold her body in half, to run from the painful grip upon her. She could smell herself, her blood, her waste, her fear.

"Tell us where they are, or it will be more than my hand that invades you," her captor hissed in her ear once more, a sick note of amusement in his dark voice.

Her throat closed and she gagged, choking on her own saliva, her own fear. For a Lapith to rape a Human was indeed worse than death, though death would come, but not before he cleaved her, mutilated her flesh in inhuman ways. It was, as he warned, worse than death.

Belamay bit her tongue. The sharp, painful jolt cleared her mind, a bit, enough.

She needed time, time to think, to plan... something.

"Release me from these chains." Her ragged voice sounded pathetic, a pleading she hoped for, not one wholly feigned. "Give me some water. I can't think... I don't remem..."

Belamay let her head fall once more to her chest. Though the metal cuffs dug harshly into her skin, she released her weight to them, as if she would drop to the floor without them.

"Don't be fooled, Kondred, she is as strong as you are," a hate-filled voice hissed nearby. In it, she heard someone she knew. Her mind scurried on the sound, but not for long.

Her chin jut, her eyes popped open. "Fosrin!" she exclaimed harshly, with shock and disgust.

Behind her, Kondred laughed. "Your mind is not that addled, I see."

The dark-haired Human who had once been Witon's second-in-command stepped closer, close enough for her to see him. What remained in her stomach from whenever she last ate or drank came readily up her throat, spewing from her mouth, spackling his pristine boots.

"Damn your Star," Fosrin spat, while Kondred laughed.

Belamay spit the bitterness off her tongue and in her mind. "By the Stars, your betrayal will see your end, Fosrin, I swear it. A painful one. And your name will forever be synonymous with 'betrayer'."

She need not play the role; the spew of hatred and vomit brought the spots back before her eyes. She dropped onto the chains once more, unable to hold herself up a moment longer. Though she tried, struggled with any strength she had left, it was for naught. Belamay felt herself fading, the blackness enfolding her once more.

* * *

Beyond the screaming in her mind, she heard their whispering, knew the voices of the Elvin brothers.

Could it be...? she wondered.

Fluttering about the camp slowly, alerting no one with the whizzing of furiously flapping wings, she hovered just above, looking, listening.

"Belamay?" Nevod fell back with the shock of his brother's word, the terror deeply etched upon Lydan's face. "What of her? Is she in danger?"

"She is, of the worst kind." Vishena buzzed in. As soon as she heard Nevod's few words, she knew Lydan had seen what she had, perhaps more.

The Queen of Faeries hovered inches from the long, straight nose of the Elf warrior. "Tell me, Lydan, and I will tell you."

"Y… you too?" Nevod brought his hands to his temples, or perhaps toward his ears.

The two seers whispered together, dark and low, their voices the shadows of nightmares.

"If it was anyone but Belamay…" Lydan's voice trailed off. He raked clawed fingers through his plaits. The thought was devastating for so many reasons.

"Do we tell him?" Vishena was now perched upon one of Lydan's knee, both of which were still pulled up to his chest.

"What could he do? He will blame himself. It will destroy him." Nevod scuttled across the sand to squat beside them.

"How can we not tell him, brother?" Lydan groaned. "If it was Zelia, and someone knew of this and did not tell…" Once more his voice trailed away, choked off by anger.

"But if we assure him we'll do all we can—"

"What? What can you do?" Nevod snipped off a harsh whisper, his sleep-messed hair alive and flopping about his head as it jerked with anger.

Lydan turned to the sprite before him; they wore the same look of worried concentration.

"The more often we make a connection with her…" Vishena began.

"…the stronger it becomes." Lydan sat up sharply, tumbling the Faerie head over end; Vishena righted herself with a quick flap of her wings.

"And the stronger it becomes, the greater the possibility grows."

"Indeed." Lydan smiled, almost. "Indeed it does."

"What does that mean?" Nevod hissed through his teeth this time, impatient with the private whisperings of the other two. "What does that do for Belamay?"

Vishena flit over to his anger-splotched face. "Dear Elf, if a telepathic connection becomes strong enough, it can become a conversation. It is why we are seeing… feeling… what is happening to her. We have been reaching out to her so much and so often, her mind is reaching back to us."

A deep furrow formed between the Elf's brows; his narrowed eyes flit between his brother and the Faerie. "And that means…?"

"It means, brother," Lydan clasped Nevod's shoulder, "that either Vishena or I may 'speak' to Belamay, show her a way out of her prison."

"Well, let's do that!" Nevod exclaimed, far too loudly.

"Shush!" came a harsh command from a bedroll not far away.

Nevod clapped a hand over his mouth and his shoulders jumped up to his ears.

"Let's do that," he said again, in a barely perceptible whisper eking out from between his long fingers.

Vishena spun around his head, sharing her glow, easing his mind as she did so.

"We should at least wait for morning," she said, returning to hover before the brothers' faces.

"Then we need wait no longer," Lydan said, standing, brushing sand from himself with one hand, while pointing to the horizon with the other. "For here it comes."

Three sets of eyes turned to the rim of tangerine kissing the sky where it bowed down to meet the earth.

* * *

She clung to her dreams as she would to a sword or to Witon. The part of Belamay's mind that was still asleep fought with that already awake, for wakefulness was the true demon of this night.

With slow movements, she tried to deny it, to keep alertness at bay by shaking her head. But it didn't shake, it rolled... it rolled on the floor.

Her dark eyes flashed open, eager now to be awake. A worthy reward greeted her.

She no longer stood upright, forced to stand with chains binding ankles and wrists. She lay on a dusty stone floor, her hands still bound, but behind her back now. She turned them, flinching with pain, but it was enough for her to recognize the feeling of hemp. Belamay curled forward, glimpsing her legs and feet. Though tightly bound, naught more than rope held both her arms and her legs.

With awkward movements and grunts of pain, she squirmed her way to a sitting position, only to encounter more pain. Her buttocks and genitals throbbed, aching where Kondred had kneaded them with angry hands.

Belamay leaned against the wall that she found mere inches from her back, relieving the brunt of the pressure for her damaged parts. As she kept her eyes open, her sight adjusted to the dimness, to the dingy room lit only by a lone, small torch perched on a wall in some distant corner. But there was light, just enough light.

With a moan of ecstasy, Belamay saw the dented tin cup, no more than half a foot away, and in it, sparkling with the reflection of that far light… water.

Belamay flopped down onto her elbows, shimmying closer to the cup and the liquid life it held within. That's when she saw the second miracle. A wooden trencher with a lone piece of bread sat just beside the cup. Now she groaned with need, not knowing which to imbibe first.

Like a worm, she scuttled to the sustenance. She took the rim of the cup in her teeth, tilting her head back… too quickly. Precious drops ran down her face, missing her mouth. As swiftly, as smoothly, as possible, she set it back down. She could not spill any. She wanted it, needed it, every drop. She must have it. With a stilling breath, she leaned down once more. With not a smidgen of shame, she lapped at it like a dog; fast, too fast. With all the strength she had left, Belamay slowed her intake, knowing it was better to take it slowly or she would only vomit again. Getting her breath back, feeling the cleanness of the water snake its way down her gullet, she turned to the plate.

Belamay looked upon the hunk of stale bread as if it were a roasted capon—her favorite food—and, like the starving creature she was, she took tiny bites, chewing slowly, savoring every scrap. Her meager meal lasted for minutes uncounted, minutes nearing ecstasy. Her stomach—empty for so long, how long she did not know—bloated with it.

Once she had finished, a thick lethargy fell upon her. Though Belamay's pains seemed eased, the image of the Lapith's face in her mind sparked stronger than ever. But she could do nothing right now save regain some semblance of physical strength. Belamay could do naught more than slump once more to the floor and release her hold on consciousness yet again.

* * *

He didn't move. For minutes untallied, Witon sat in stony silence. His full lips hung open, his breath huffed, and his silver eyes jumped like a cricket from one face to another.

Lydan spared a quick glance at Vishena, seeing his own confused concern on her beautiful countenance.

"Witon, do you understand what we ha—"

The blood-curdling scream rent the air. Witon jumped up with it... spinning first in one direction, then the other. Turning so fast, his body appeared inhuman, un-controlled. He thrashed away from them, then back. He grabbed his hair and pulled, skin plying off his skull.

"Witon, please…" Vishena tried to stop him.

With nowhere to place his anger, she feared he would injure himself.

He growled at her, dark and thunderous. Vishena flit away; she had never seen such anguish.

Yet somehow, some way, he hurt no one, not even him-self.

Another growl, a grunt, then he bent down and lifted the stump that had been his chair.

His arms were not long enough to fit fully round it, so large it was, so heavy it must be. Yet lift it he did. With a scream that laid waste to all others, he hurled the wood away from him… feet from him… as if to do so, somehow discharged his pain, his rage.

Yet Witon did not move. He stood seething with fury and bereavement. His chest expanded and collapsed with each hefted breath.

"What is it, Witon? My Stars, are you injured?" Mitren rushed toward his brother, sun-ruddy skin blanched to the color of the sand he ran across. "Witon, brother, what—"

Nevod jumped up and jumped between them, fearful in case Witon should hurl his anger upon his brother, know-ing that, at times, only with a brother can one do such a thing.

"Wait, wait," he whispered to Mitren, pushing hard against the firm chest, the large Human matching the strength of the Elf in his need to get to his sibling.

"Leave me be, Nevod. Witon needs—"

"He needs a few moments," Nevod said, as if that somehow it served as an explanation. "Just a few more. Sit. Sit down, Mitren."

Brown eyes, dark now and deep, almost as eerie as his brother's, scoured the Elf's face. Whatever he looked for, he found. With cautious compliance, he sat beside Lydan. Vishena whirled to him, lighting upon his shoulder.

Witon's breathing slackened; they could see it in the slower and slower rise of his shoulders. But he did not turn. When they heard his soft sobs, they understood.

"Now, Mitren," Vishena whispered. "He needs you now."

Mitren jumped up, no more prodding needed, nor explanations.

He crossed to his brother and wrapped his muscular arms around his sibling's quivering body. Like that, they stood, and the sight of Witon's quiet tears broke every heart within hearing.

As morning aged, as crew members woke, they began to draw near. But one look at the Man whom all loved, found them turning away. Though curious, though fearful, their respect demanded they give him his privacy. They could do no more for him than those already with him had done.

The sharp scent of burning wood filled the air, vying with the briny scent of the sea, followed soon by the enticing aroma of burning meat. The camp came to life. Mitren held on.

At last, Witon lifted his head from Mitren's shoulder.

The brothers began to whisper, the kind of private talk that siblings shared. No doubt Witon told Mitren all. Or all he knew.

"Come back, dear sirs." Vishena floated up in the circle of stumps that had become, in its most primitive form, the Council Chamber. "Come and let us tell you now, what we plan to do."

"*Do?*" Witon shook his head as if to clear it. Pinching the bridge of his nose with thumb and forefinger, wiping tear streaks from his cheeks with the back of his hands, Witon became, once more, Human. "There is something you can do?"

The Faerie flew to him, landing on his shoulder, embracing his face with her arms and her wings, closing her eyes with the tightness of it.

"There is always something one can do, always."

With the two of them explaining, it took little time for Vishena and Lydan to convey their plan.

In the wake of their recitation, Witon sat in silence once more, but not for long. When he broke it, he did so with two words.

"Begin... now."

Chapter XVII

JUSTICE IN ANY LAND IS JUST

First, one day passed, and then the next. Each time, it became harder and harder for the two seers to face Witon, to see his face, once full of hope, fall to despair.

"You must get more rest," Flerial tutted to her Queen, as she administered to the exhausted Faerie Queen's head, plying a compost to relieve the aches.

Gently but insistently, Vishena pushed the nursing hands away, with a shake of her head.

"No, no. I will not rest until she is safe."

They all knew. By now, the whole camp knew of Belamay's capture and what was being done to save her. Most steered clear of Witon, as well as Vishena and Lydan, dealing with them only when they must, and even then, they would seek out other members of the Council first. Those that did approach Witon did so only to tell them of their prayers to the Stars. Each time he would thank them, with genuine gratitude, and each time their heartfelt concern brought an ache to his heart.

Vishena turned with a hard stare to Flerial. "How can I even rest while she endures such torment?"

Without waiting for an answer, the Queen of the Faeries took flight again, with little concern for the darkness quickly falling on another day, shimmering away in the growing gloom.

She flew higher, faster, than she had ever done before. Her small, perfect body thrummed with energy, with every range of emotion, from anger, to fear, to heartwrenching concern. Vishena flew farther from camp then she ever had, not realizing she no longer recognized the terrain speeding by below her. That's when it happened, when she looked down.

Even in the dark, she could usually feel them coming, whatever type of impediment rose before her, even if she couldn't truly see it. But not this time. This time, the tree rose up in front of Vishena too quickly, before she could react.

Crashing into its thick, prickly trunk, Vishena flopped downward from leaf to leaf to leaf, thanking the Stars for their rough assistance downward, for without them she would have landed far too hard upon the ground, so high had she been flying. Still, the collision with the ground came none too softly.

Her head tottered on her shoulders; Vishena had lost her sense of balance as well as her flight. Grabbing it between her hands, she sat still until the dizziness passed. When it did, she looked around in the murky night.

Vishena sat in a valley; a meadowed valley filled with blooms. Even in the dark, their redolence gave them away. With squinted eyes, she could see tall mountains to her south and gently sloping hills to her north. Vishena thought she heard water gurgling, but whether from a river or the ocean she could not tell. She knew only that—

"Belamay!" Vishena yelled the name, for there she was, never more strongly, never more powerfully in her mind than in that instant.

* * *

"Belamay!"

The scream of her pain pierced her stupor.

Belamay picked up her head, feeling a dollop of blood drip from her bruised and battered nose. The torture had continued, she knew not for how long. All she knew, the only hope she clung to, was that Kondred had not yet taken her. It would be his last act; one she would never survive, and they both knew it. Her saving grace was that dead, she served him not a whit.

Peering into the darkness, she saw no one, yet the sound of her name being called echoed still in her mind. Her lids dropped, closing, but not of their own accord. With her eyelids shut, she finally 'saw' who called her from out of the darkness.

"Vishena!" A beseeching sob, one of hope and relief. "Help me, dear Vishena."

Vishena did.

With images so distinct, so real that they frightened Belamay, Vishena allowed Belamay to see behind her own back, to see the cords holding her hands and the knot keeping them bound.

Slowly, excruciatingly slowly, through the darkest part of the night, they worked together for hours; together, they unbound the ropes. The pure physical ecstasy of their release brought Belamay to tears, great sobs that shook her shoulders as she rubbed tenderly at the raw skin where first the chains, then the ropes had been.

Your legs, dear Belamay, set them free.

She was so relieved to have her hands unbound, Belamay could not think clearly; Vishena did her thinking for her. With trembling, bloody fingers, Belamay untied the ropes from her ankles, lavishing them with the same tender caresses as she had her wrists. In the bliss of it, came more thoughts from Vishena. Belamay shook her head at them, tears flying off her face.

"No, no, I must—"

"You *must!*" Vishena raised her 'voice,' ordering Belamay, quickly 'explaining' why, until finally, Belamay understood and started following Vishena's contrary instructions.

As her breath hitched with more sobs, Belamay wrapped the bindings once more about her ankles and wrists, but they were loosely wrapped, not tied. With them once more behind her back, with her back once more propped against the wall, Belamay closed her eyes. She knew she had no chance of sleep, but at least she could rest. She might be free of the bindings, but there lay only one way out of the cell. She would need her strength.

Belamay heard the creature's approach, as she had more times than she cared to count. But this time she heard Vishena's 'voice' as well, and it made all the difference. She sat as still as a Stone Giant, her chin to her chest, her shoulders slumped. The keys jangled in the lock. The door creaked open. Belamay allowed her eyes, opened to no more than slits, to slither sideways for a look. With control she thought no longer hers, she gave no outward sign of the depth of her thankful prayers, nor of those she 'heard' Vishena make as well.

By some stroke of luck, or perhaps of Vishena's magic, or that which they made together, it was no monster, nor monstrous creature that came, but a Human male, and a puny one at that.

Belamay barely lifted her head as he approached with her daily ration of bread and water. Lifting her bruised face as he neared, she allowed—for the first time—the true depth of her pain and fear, to show. Belamay became the personification of vulnerable helplessness.

The man snickered. "Ah, so the great female warrior is not so great, after all."

The taint of disgust as his tongue spoke of her sex told Belamay all she needed to know about this man; his prejudice flowed in many directions.

Dropping the plate of meager sustenance on the floor, he stood before her, taking his fill of the sight of her half-exposed breasts. Unlike the others, he did not stand behind her to untie her hands, to allow her a few moments to eat. Instead, he crouched down in front of her, his face within a foot of hers. Before reaching behind her, he reached in her shirt, squeezing one breast with harsh cruelty.

Belamay could see the ugly lust in his eyes.

"No true warrior has these; they are only toys for those of us who are."

"You… you are a true warrior?" Belamay allowed every ounce of exhaustion and humility to pulse in her voice, but not a trace of her anger. That she held onto tightly.

"Indeed I am, mistress."

Releasing his hold on her, he skipped to the small aperture in the rough-hewn door, looked about and, seeing what he hoped to see, or not, he closed and locked the door. All was empty and silent, save for the two of them.

Returning to her, he squatted down once more. "I believe I shall show you just how powerful I am."

He took his eyes from her, directing his attention to the laces of his breeches where his hands fluttered.

"No," Belamay said, a flat condemnation. "I'll show you."

Whipping her hands around, she grabbed the man by the back of the neck, yanking his head toward hers as she flung her own forward.

Their skulls collided, the point of her hairline—the hardest part of the skull—connecting with the bridge of his nose, right between his eyes.

Instantly, blood spurt from his nostrils. His eyes rolled in their sockets and he staggered back.

Belamay braced her hands on the floor and, with all her strength, lifted both her legs up, ramming them out and into his stomach.

The man doubled over, gasping for breath, falling sideways onto the stone floor as he held his battered gut.

Belamay reached down, grabbed his keys and his sword and turned toward the door. She'd gained her freedom in seconds, but she would spare just a few more.

Standing over him, she cocked one leg back like a catapult and released her foot straight into his genitals with all the hate and anger simmering deep within.

"You'll not be using that weapon anytime soon, oh... great... warrior," Belamay taunted him, then spat on him, as she would all those who had taken her, if she could.

He groaned and wailed with pain, so she kicked him again, in the mouth, a knockout strike.

With a smile and a sniff of laughter, Belamay opened the cell door and peered down each end of the corridor. She saw no one, but she did see light; the light of freedom.

* * *

The jolt brought him awake with a searing, harsh gasp through his lungs.

Lydan bolted up, swirling in a whirl of sand, unsure which way to go in the darkness.

"Brother?" Nevod moaned sleepily, cracking open his lids.

Seeing Lydan stumbling about, he knew.

Nevod pushed behind his shoulders, flinging himself up from his back to his feet, and grabbed his brother.

Together, like children with hands clasped, they ran to Witon.

Though still a few feet from their friend's bedroll, Lydan fell upon his knees, scurrying the rest of the way to the Man's side.

"Witon, Witon." With hands like biting claws, he shook Witon and called his name till the Man came awake.

Seeing the Elf, seeing the night sky filled with stars, Witon knew a moment had come... but which would it be? He could not bring himself to ask.

"She lives, Witon," Lydan said, his voice catching on tears of joy. "She is free and she lives."

Witon gasped, a jagged, wrenching sound. Between sobs, he could say but a few words. "Oh, thank thee... Great Stars. I thank thee... with my life."

He flung himself forward then, into the arms of the Elvin brothers. Together, they cried, droplets of pure joy.

* * *

He had taken to his bed almost as early as the sun had.

But not before checking and rechecking everything.

Tomorrow would find Fosrin on the battlefield, yet again. But this time, for the first time, he would be the commander. He would call the order; he would order the deaths.

Fosrin's heart yammered at him in excitement. It had taken all the strength he had to calm himself, to free his mind with thoughts of the coming carnage, and drift off into a deep sleep. But sleep he did, so deeply, he did not hear the creak of the shutters as they slowly opened, or the light footfalls on the rushes just steps from where he lay.

Only in the last instant of his life did he wake... to see her face just above his—her teeth clenched, her lips tight in a maleficent grin—to feel her blade against his throat.

"Don—"

It was the last sound he made on this Earth before the blade slashed across his throat, before his life's blood pumped out and soaked the linens about him.

She watched, perhaps longer than she should have done, but as long as she must, ignoring the quivering, urging hiss from the one who held the ladder to the embrasure. She had to see the vacant glare of lifeless eyes before she could turn away, before knowing that her work was well and truly done.

"Now, m'lady. You must come away now."

She turned then, wiping her blade clean on the dead man's linens, brushing the splatters of blood from her face with the back of her hand.

"Yes, Josem. Now I can leave."

* * *

"It's been hours, My Lord." Flerial buzzed about his head, her concern bright in the flash of her wings.

Witon's joy at hearing of Belamay's freedom burst at the news of Vishena's disappearance. Hearing of her last words to Flerial made his heart pound heavily with guilt. If she had not been so determined to reach Belamay, to free her, she would have been safe in her wee bed the whole of the night.

He clasped his brother on the shoulder. "Gather twelve of the best scouts. Send them out in groups of three. We must—"

"You must do nothing at all."

At the sound of Vishena's voice, Witon spun round, nearing knocking Mitren off his feet. If he could have wrapped her in his arms, he would have done so. Instead, he settled for opening his palm, delighting in her warmth as she landed there, bringing his hand—and the Faerie—close to his cheek in the best embrace there could be between a Man and a Faerie. As Vishena leaned her tiny, fragile, exhausted body against his face, each creature closed their eyes with the solace of it.

"Never again, Vishena," Witon grumbled, his relief turning to testiness as fear for a loved one can so often do. He held her only inches from his silvery eyes, eyes bright with emotion. "I know you are a Queen, I know you are accustomed to having your own way, but we are in a strange land. You cannot just go flitting off, especially at night."

The normally bright auburn glow of the leader of the Faerie nation turned dark, brownish, as her small chin dropped and her shoulders slumped. "Witon, I—"

"I will not listen to excuses..." Witon chided.

"And I was not going to give any," Vishena confessed, surprising all who heard. "It was incautious of me, and I know it. It will never happen again."

"I... uh... well then." Witon stumbled on this resolute creature's quick contriteness.

"I can only say this," Vishena continued, lifting off his palm to flutter in the air. "A force came upon me that was so strong, I could not deny it. Belamay's force."

She had his attention then, not to chide but to listen. Vishena held them all spellbound as she described the burst of Belamay's consciousness in Vishena's mind. She told them of the connection made between them in the moment—one more than telepathic, one both physical and cerebral—of Belamay's tenacity and bravery, of Vishena's fall, and ultimately Belamay's freedom.

Witon reached behind him as his legs quivered. As his knees buckled, he reached for one of the large rocks in the circle that had become the rustic, but first Council Chamber of this new world.

His mind whirled with possibilities, great and small, horrific and harrowing, magnificent and blessed. He shook his head at the deluge of them, finally looking up, mindless of the other members of the Council that had heard the rumble of voices and came rushing toward them.

"How can I ever thank you? How can I ever repay you?" One lone tear ran a straight course down one sharp-boned cheek as he looked up to Vishena.

"My dear Man, you need thank me no more than you already have." The Faerie buzzed to light upon his shoulder. "She means a great deal to me as well… to all of us."

She swept her small arm out to include the gathering around them, a gesture met with grunts and chirps of agreement, a harmonic concord of abiding truth.

Witon swallowed and his throat bobbed on the clog of emotion. "Upon the Stars, Vishena, whatever you need, whenever you need me, I am at your service, now and forever."

Vishena smiled softly, a wisp of both love and indulgence. "As you would have been, no matter the outcome."

Witon shrugged his shoulders; he could not deny it. He was devoted to her—to every creature who had made this journey—as if they were his blood kin, and he always would be.

With a flutter about his head, the still grinning Faerie started away, only to quickly buzz back.

"There is one request I would make, if I may?" She spoke to him and to the group as well.

"Anything," Witon answered quickly, backed by a chorus of agreement from every creature present.

"I know where I would like the Faerie Village to be," Vishena announced, without explanation. She needed none.

"Of course," Witon decreed. "It is done."

Once more, words of acquiescence filled the air.

The Council settled in, on the rocks in the circle about the fire which was now firmly stoked and warming, thanks to Mitren. Something held them together, perhaps more than one thing.

Jwara, with her sweetness, finally gave voice to it.

"Do you think, my dear," she asked, her voice smooth and soft, thick with natural sweetness, "that you will be able to do it again? Do you think you will be able to... to bond with Belamay so powerfully again?"

It was *the* question; the only one that mattered now Belamay was safe. Their survival—along with the very existence of this New World—depended on those remaining on Minra Enra to know to make their own way; to realize that the ship would not be coming back to lead them here.

Witon held his breath as he kept his gaze upon Vishena's beautiful wee face, as her small, perfect eyes traveled the circle of creatures around her. He let it out with a huff, shoulders slouching at the barely perceptible shake of her head.

"I... I do not know," she answered and in her quiet tone, her uncertainty blared. "I have never felt such a powerful connection with a Human before. I'm not sure if its strength came from the ghastliness of her situation or if there is something stronger between us."

Silence laid a heavy shroud upon them even as the sky began to change its clothes, shedding its gown of night for a brighter dress of day.

"But I do know this." Vishena broke the silence, all hesitancy and doubt banished now. "I will not stop trying. I will continue to reach out to Belamay and to others, until our message is heard."

"As will I," Lydan decreed and with their certitude, all found once more what they needed most of all... faith.

Chapter XVIII

A COUNTRY IS BORN

Their settlement grew swiftly, beautifully, beyond Witon's hopes or dreams. It took but a few days to transfer all the supplies, wood, and stores to their permanent campsite in the teardrop-shaped section of land at the southern tip of the continent. The crew and the Council, working arduously side by side, erected a few shelters from the materials left from the Freedom and as they worked in the forest, they gathered materials to build more.

For the time being, the crew shared two large, half-walled, tent-like cabins among them, while Witon and Mitren lived with Nevod and Lydan, the Brownies with the Trolls and the Dwarves with the Faeries. Only the Centaurs remained without a structure.

"We have always lived among the trees," Chiron told Witon. "We need nothing more than what this bountiful land can offer us."

The mighty Centaurs spent their waking hours in camp, working as hard as the others, but at night they traveled into the trees just north of the home site.

"I have never slept so well in my life," Chalene told the Council, as they took a mid-day meal together, the sun a diffused peach behind thin, creamy clouds, the air redolent and warm, her large face bright with pleasure. "To know I can close my eyes with no fear of spies or hunters, has brought me a greater serenity than I have ever imagined."

"I have even heard her snoring," her brother teased, as brothers are wont to do, while the gathering laughed, merrily returning to their work.

And there was so much to do.

Wood was available in abundance and the ease of the move inspired almost fanatical dedication. Efforts began with felling trees, with a cautious eye to where clearings would do them the most good and where re-growth was sure to sprout. Each tree sacrificed—many of such wood as never seen before, wood of deep red or pale yellow—was noted and showered with thoughts of gratitude as the workers turned those trees into usable wood. With their limited tools, each piece of wood became a plank, which became a piece of a permanent structure. Each creature worked to their own special talents, the larger men felling the trees while others toiled at carving and smoothing.

Jwara, Flerial, and Glasion spent their time together foraging through the woods for healing herbs. Their stores of catalogued plants grew daily, and were immediately put to use as the minor cuts, scrapes, and pulled muscles became more and more abundant as the New World began to take shape. The three healers took turns staffing the makeshift medical station, while the others slept or foraged.

The Centaurs assisted the cutting crew, using their incredible strength to haul the downed trees back to camp, where Uganta and Turatan worked with those finishing the lumber. Nevod and the Brownies counted themselves among the hunters and food providers, spending hours tracking the strange wild beasts roaming the land, or fishing in the river that ran past the camp on both sides. Climora had never seen Brasher work so hard when they'd lived on Minra Enra, and she said so, whenever the Council came together for the end of the day meal, a tradition started by mere happenstance and one quickly treasured.

Swerin took little time in forming a temporary forge, erecting a square of large stones standing two feet high and a perfect four-foot square. Gathering all the pieces of brass and steel salvaged from the *Freedom's* remains, the delighted Dwarf began to make the tools necessary for building their new home. Precious, all-too-few shovels and lathes, rakes and trowels became gifts for the cheering workers from the humble but satisfied Dwarf.

Though they longed to get their hands dirty—to be among those who laid the foundation of their new world—there was far too much administrative work for Witon and Persky. Inventories must be kept, as well as an accounting of each day's progress, and the sick and injured list must be updated daily. Though no longer at sea, Witon continued to make entries in his log every day as well, so when the others came...

When, he thought, *always think when...*

...so when the others came, he would be able to tell them everything... so their world would have a record of its beginning.

As the waiting stretched on, Witon couldn't help but notice the hidden looks and hopeful expressions aimed toward Lydan and Vishena. Though Man and Creature grew strong and healthy, muscles hardened and faces glowed with so many kisses of the sun, Witon saw their eyes wander to these two and wonder at the progress of their own work. Yet no one dared ask.

Some were afraid of the answer, and yet their hearts and minds constantly battled between thoughts of their loved ones and the true future of their new land.

Vishena and Lydan concentrated on their mental communications every day and for hours at a time. Lydan sat under a tree not very far from the core of work. Hour after hour he would sit, eyes closed in deep concentration. Vishena took flight so often these days, she was hardly ever in camp, returning only for the evening meal, when she forced down a few morsels of food and soon fell fast asleep.

Witon could find no fault with the others and their obsession, as he was, himself, obsessed. He ordered a man to be posted around the clock, one at each of the two natural harbors. At this very moment, he made a crude estimation of when the others would arrive if Lydan and Vishena's efforts were successful.

Captain's Log, Twenty-Sixth day of the First Spring Moon, Fourteen Hundred Twelve.

If successful communication between Lydan and Vishena and their loved ones occurred on the first day's effort, it should take Belamay and Zelia approximately two weeks to gather the others. It would take at least two more weeks for them to procure a proper vessel, if, Oh Good Stars please, there was one available, then at least two more weeks for them to purchase all the goods and stores required and get them on board. Assuming all takes place accordingly, an additional three to four days would be required for the journey itself. Therefore 'twill be six weeks and six days until they arrive. To date, two weeks and four days have passed.

Witon could write no more. His hand trembled and the scar on the back of his head ached. He threw down paper and quill and strode off to join the others at work.

Days passed and their efforts soon showed tremendous results. Every manner of creature had their own cabin and the crewmembers were able to erect lodgings of their own, or one to share with a friend if they did not prefer a more solitary life. A dining hall appeared, one large enough to hold and feed everyone comfortably, as well as space for a roomy cooking area with two large stone fireplaces. A permanent Medical Facility arose, with shelf after shelf of remedies and medications, and an entire structure now existed to house the growing food stores.

These days, the pilgrims worked on building a fortification around the entire camp. They'd not thought they required one until the morning when Granler, the ship's cook, now the camp's head chef, awoke and discovered the ransacked food bin from which half the provisions had vanished, pilfered by hungry animals. The construction of the fence was one of the last chores their camp required and the men took their time, carving intricate patterns on the wood's face and the elaborate pilings for the corner posts.

Captain's Log, Twenty-Eighth day of the Second Spring Moon, Fourteen Hundred Twelve

Work continues on the fortification. Unfortunately, this only requires but a few men. There is no more that can be done, needs to be done, without the additional supplies coming to us with the next boat and the loved ones it will carry. The inactivity wreaks havoc on us all.

It has been seven weeks and one day since Lydan and Vishena began their attempts at communication with those back on Minra Enra. Either their communications have not succeeded, or it is taking longer than I anticipated for them to reach us... or worse.

The possibility that the others aren't coming, combined with the aforementioned inactivity, has brought everyone's nerves to the breaking point. Just this very morning I was required to disrupt a fistfight between two crewmembers. 'Twas doubly disturbing as these two particular men have been friends for many years and their quarrel centered on a matter of great insignificance. Upon conclusion of this entry,

I must act as judge at an adjudication where I must decide not only on guilt and innocence, but the proper punishment.

The other Council members are endeavoring to keep themselves hopeful and busy by exploring this great land of ours, in an effort to locate and designate suitable areas for villages for their own species. Presently, Swerin and Jwara, Brasher and Climora are away from camp on just such a reconnaissance mission.

Witon wished for more to write, anything to keep him from the dining hall and the court he must preside over, but his thoughts were too doom-filled to include. With great reluctance, he put log and quill away and began to make his way to the dining hall. No sooner did he step outside his hut's door, than Lydan joined him. Together, they trod upon the path, a dirt-packed road forming by the natural movements of the inhabitants of the small village.

"Are ye ready for your first try as arbiter?"

"Nay, not really." Witon's head pointed to the ground and his shoulders slumped over like that of an old man. "Who am I to judge others and their actions?"

"You are the natural one to do so. You are our leader. We all look to you for guidance."

"I am the ship's Captain and the ship is in ruins."

Lydan stopped and grabbed Witon by the shoulder, halting him as well.

"You are a great deal more than that, sir." Lydan's honey-green eyes peered deeply into Witon's silver ones, never letting the connection waver. "Thou art the dreamer whose hopes have become our reality. You are the spark upon which this fire of freedom feeds. You have made the outlandish possibility of living in freedom a truth."

"'Twas destined to happen, with or without me."

"Your power is much greater than ye think."

Witon raised a foot to take a step, stopped, and lowered it back down.

"What is that supposed to mean?" Witon's eyes narrowed at the Elf before him.

Lydan looked around and saw a fairly deserted encampment; no doubt everyone, save those working on the fence, was already in the dining hall to witness the first court session. He pulled Witon over to a hut boasting a small, benched sitting area in its front space. The quietness of the normally busy village surrounded them as they sat. The lusty, warm breeze brought the bright scent of flowers from the surrounding meadows and picked up the men's long hair, tossing it about playfully.

"There have been some Council meetings that you are unaware of," Lydan began and held up a hand to stop Witon's protests before they began. "They were about you, and that is why you were not part of them."

"About *me*?" Witon yelped, thunderstruck, not only at hearing that the Council had met without him, but that he had been the topic of their discussions.

Lydan heaved a heavy sigh, a breath of 'now or never.'

"A unanimous decision has been made. We believe you should serve as this land's first king."

"Hah!" Witon started to laugh, his mirth turning into a croak as he realized he spoke to Lydan, not the mischievous Nevod.

"Are ye serious?"

"Completely."

Witon stared at the creature in absolute silence. Lydan returned his stare with unwavering certainty. Witon scratched his head, then rubbed his face with both hands as if washing it without benefit of soap or water.

"You, what about you? The Council of Creatures was your conception," Witon accused. "Why do you not take the lead? You are one of the most compassionate and empathetic creatures I have ever met. Yours is the voice of truth. Few are as trusted as deeply as you. You—"

"I... I am not forceful enough." Lydan turned on the bench to face Witon straight on. "A king must be both diplomat and warrior, as are you."

"But I would not, could not, be your typical king," Witon whispered from behind a hand that cupped his head in disbelief. "This land's very purpose is to establish a unique way of life, with a different form of government, with the Council establishing its rules and laws."

"That you would not be typical, we have no doubt, which is precisely why you should be king. And, yes, the Council will decide the rules but there must be someone, some pivotal point of authority to carry out those rules. Besides," Lydan's face split in a wiry grin, "no one else wants the job."

"The Council speaks for its creatures," Witon shook his head slowly back and forth, "Dwarves, Brownies, Trolls, Centaurs, Faeries, and Elves, but who speaks for the Humans?"

"Your brother is part of the Council, is he not? He is Human, no?"

Witon laughed once again.

"I didn't always think so, growing up with him, but aye, he is Human."

Lydan smiled, knowing all too well the strange emotions running between brothers. "Then his is the voice of the Humans. He even went so far as to survey the crew to see if he spoke correctly for them."

"And...?"

"And once more," Lydan nodded emphatically, "the decision was unanimous."

Again, Witon just stared at his companion.

"Can ye give me some time, time to think about... all this?"

"Of course!" Lydan stood and pulled Witon to his feet. "Take all the time ye want, just know that we will accept no answer save yes."

This time, as Witon's mouth gaped and his eyes bulged, Lydan did laugh, slapping the stunned Man on the back as they once more took up their journey along the path. Together, the two comrades strode in silence to the dining hall. As the door opened, the creatures inside saw Witon entering... and all rose to their feet.

"See?" whispered Lydan in Witon's ear. "Already they treat you as their king."

Witon could but look skeptically over one shoulder at Lydan as he made his way to the front of the room and the table and chair set up for him there. He listened intently as both sides made their case and listened more keenly than ever, knowing everyone looked to him not as their captain, but as their king. He knew, too, that Katrin drew the scene with different strokes.

He gleaned quickly that much of the action of these men erupted from nervous energy... the lack of women and their soothing company, the worry that none of their kind would ever come and each breed would slowly die out. He took his time deliberating over each man's testimony and, when he finally made the decision known, the assemblage applauded him for his fair and equitable verdict.

Lydan watched as the crowd cheered their leader. As they filed out of the room, any divisiveness knitted and healed. In their murmured conversations, their genial and satisfied expressions, there was nothing to see if not a greater fealty toward each other, and especially Witon.

Witon watched Lydan studying the assemblage. Lydan turned and caught Witon's eye and, try though he might, the Elf could not erase the very pleased, almost smug smile from his face. With an innocent shrug, Lydan left Witon alone, the large Man feeling meek and humble in the vast, now empty room.

He sat back down, his eyes vacantly focused on the abandoned tables and chairs, his mind wandering leagues away. Outside, hammering resumed as the men continued to work on the fence, their voices murmuring like a babbling brook in the distance. He smelled the still fresh scent of the wooden tables and chairs, the very walls of the building he sat in, and the residual smells of a breakfast not long ago eaten and cleaned up. Witon watched as long morning shadows receded and changed to those with the short legs of midday, bringing form to elusive time and, in the space, a thousand thoughts crammed their way into his mind.

Could I really be a king? Would I be a good one? Does Belamay want to be queen? Do our children and their children and their children wish to be rulers?

These were selfish thoughts concerned only with the effects upon him and his, and he knew it. Had he really worked hard all these years to consider only his own needs and desires now?

No, he answered himself, *no. This is not just for me and those of my blood, but for all creatures who have the right to live in peaceful freedom.*

Freedom. It was the name of the vessel that brought them here. It was the very conceptual thinking that had ruled his life for more than two decades. It must be the only consideration worth any merit.

If the Stars deem me to be their instrument of freedom, then so be it.

"Persky!" Witon bellowed without any further hesitation, knowing the loyal creature was never so far away that he wouldn't hear his voice. As expected, it took but a moment for the sprite to pop his head into the doorway.

"Aye, My Lord?"

"Would you ask the Council members in camp to join me here?"

"Of course, My Lord." Persky retreated from the doorway, his hopeful eyes lingering for an inquisitive moment on his master's face.

The Council members assembled quickly, not a one having ventured far from the place of the morning's deliberations.

Every Council member came, even the Dwarves and the Brownies who had returned only moments before. Witon was pleased to see them at camp once more and, though he knew it would seem like a deliberate delay, he could not help but ask what they had discovered on their explorations.

The map came out and the Dwarves and Brownies took turns in showing the areas where they wished to make their villages. The Dwarves chose a section of mountain range that seemed to split the landmass in half horizontally.

"These mountains are as beautiful as any I've ever seen," Swerin reported. "They will make the perfect front door for our village."

Witon nodded; the entrance to many a Dwarf village could be found in the mountains' sides, while the village itself lay deep beneath them. Dwarves believed Earth's power emanated from its very core and they preferred to live as close to that core as possible.

"There were the most massive trees imaginable," began Brasher. "No, I do not speak the truth. I could never have imagined trees of such majesty existed!" Brasher squeaked, as he walked upon the map to stand at a forest between the mountain range and a hilly section near the northernmost point of the land, his small body appearing as if it were a living part of the chart. "We will have the most splendid village in all Brownie history."

Climora stood at Witon's feet and looked up at him with unfettered adoration.

"This place... this land ye have brought us to, is..." she began, but words failed her. "Thank ye," was all she could say and, with Turatan's help, she took her place atop the table next to Brasher.

"Which makes me wonder," Turatan said, brown, bloodshot eyes bright with excitement, "what shall we name this wonderful land? 'Tis about time it had a name of its own."

"That depends," Lydan spoke for the first time since the meeting came to order, "on our friend's decision." He looked then to Witon, as did all the others.

The beseeching gazes grew sharp and pointy, and Witon longed for the next moment to begin.

He filled his lungs quickly and said, "If it is what ye wish, I will be king."

The poignancy of his simple statement and the conviction with which he spoke refused to be denied.

"Huzzah!" The cheer came instantaneously, unanimously, and thunderously. The group only returned to calm at Witon's insistence and, even then, with a great deal of handshaking and hugging.

"I believe it important, however," Witon continued, touching the gaze of each with his own steely silver one, "that the announcement should not be made until the next ship arrives. If…"

"*When* it does—" Lydan cut Witon off, knowing the depth of Witon's worry and despair over the late arrival of their loved ones and the personal responsibility he felt, "—there will be a proper coronation and celebration."

"Huzzah!"

Once again, the Council erupted in cheering and congratulations amongst themselves.

"King Witon," Vishena said, buzzing over to his shoulder, taking post at one of her favorite places. "King Witon, ruler of all…"

"Yes," Turatan spoke again, "which brings us back to the name."

"That has been answered for us as well," said Lydan. "As kingdoms have for hundreds of years, 'twill be named for its founder and king."

"Of course, of course!" The group shared their astonishment over the obvious.

"You j... jest, surely?" Witon stuttered, standing so fast he upturned his chair, sending Vishena flying frantically in the empty air. "You mean to name it after me?"

"Of course." Lydan turned from his brother's embrace, one brow raised high upon his forehead. "This land must have a name and its name ought to be that of its first king."

"But... but..." Witon stammered.

"This land's birth, this new way of living, is also wrought by your hands. All the more reason to name this land for you."

"But..." Witon tried again.

"The Kingdom of Witon," Chiron piped up, dark cheeks flushing bright. "It has a nice ring to it."

"The Kingdom of Witonia." Chalene pranced as she put a lyrical spin on the word.

"Ah, even better!" Jwara clapped her pudgy hands in delight.

"Witonia, the land of Freedom," cried Uganta, a hairy fist raised triumphantly over his head.

"Witonia." Lydan spoke the word as he would the name of his child. "All those in favor?"

"Aye!" boomed the rousing chorus.

"All those opposed?"

Silence.

"Then, my fellow creatures of Witonia, to our King and our country!"

"To King and Country!" they roared and the hand-clasping and embracing resumed. Not a creature was spared in the sharing of affection. Chalene brought her enormous head down to Chiron and the Brownie put her tiny hand upon the nose that stretched longer than she was tall.

Like a buoy in the midst of a spirited sea, Witon stood immobilized as the revelry whirled around him. He remained frozen in this extreme moment as Mitren strode to the door and called to the cook—waiting patiently just beyond the door—to begin the midday meal.

"Make it special, cooky," Mitren instructed, his limitless pride in his brother transforming his usual meekness to bravado.

Witon remained motionless; a stone pillar in a busy and crowded marketplace, watching as the room filled with the cooking crew and the Council members took celebration in a glass of ale, dipping into the almost depleted ration of it.

"But I never intended for this to happen. I never intended to be king," he said in a quiet whisper, not knowing if anyone listened.

"And if being king had been your intention," Nevod whispered in Witon's ear, "it never would have happened at all."

Nevod slapped Witon jovially on the back and made for the ale.

Witon sat back down, some might say fell, and he looked out the window and up into the sparkling violet firmament. "Papa? Papa, can you hear me? Papa, I am… a king."

Chapter XIX

THERE BE MAGIC HERE

She sat at her small table, long after the banked fire began its slow dimming, as the stars grew bright in the firmament, and her eyes squinted to see her own work.

The scene that day in the great hall, the picture of Witon—*King* Witon, Katrin corrected herself with a small smile—had affected her so deeply that she continued to work on the vision of it she had captured in her mind, rendered on the large parchment before her. No detail was too small; not the intensity with which every creature had hung on King Witon's words, nor the white of the king's knuckles as he presided over his first arbitration, nor the satisfied look upon the face of the lovely Lydan. Katrin could not have known then what wrought that smile, only that she must capture it.

Her hands flew over the parchment, as if they knew, more than she, what lines needed to be where, what shading and softening was required to give the picture dimensionality, depth… realism.

"ZZZ-Zzzz-ZZzzz-hngGGggh-Ppbhww- zZZzzzZZ…."

Katrin sniffed a laugh, marveling at the sounds the small Brownie made in her sleep.

As more and more cabins were built, as more and more choices for living arrangements were made, Katrin could have had her choice of them—as the only female Human—and whether to inhabit it alone. She had chosen a cozy, smallish, two-room structure, perched near the cabins occupied by the many crewman. No bigotry lived in the choice, only the sense of familiarity it gave her to be near Men.

Living alone, being alone, however, was not a life she would choose. Having been raised in a household of three sisters and two brothers, noise and chaos had been a constant companion, one she had grown to love and cherish. But, as the only female Human, her choices of living partner were limited. How thankful she felt then when Climora had approached her, sheepishly so for a Brownie, asking if Katrin would care to share her homestead.

"No offense against dear Brasher," the wee sprite had said softly as she stood upon the table where Katrin sat in the main hall at the evening meal one night, "but... but... well, he simply does not stop talking... *ever!*"

How Katrin had laughed at the small, but exaggerated, exasperated toss-up of Climora's wee hands. She had said yes without hesitation.

More than one night passed as this one did, with Katrin, in the main room serving as a small kitchen—should they choose a quiet, private meal—as well as a den, where she often worked at the finely crafted table Lusby had provided them. While in the next chamber, a small bed-room with one large feather mattress and one quite small, Climora snorted, grunted, and snuffled her way through the land of dreams. Though disharmonic, Katrin had quickly learned to sleep through the Brownie's sounds; so, like the noises of crickets and other insects of the night, they soon came to soothe her.

Katrin put down her charcoal, rubbing her hands to-gether to rid them of any trace of the fine, black residual they left, before rubbing her face and the fatigue behind her eyes. How blessed it felt to close them for a moment.

That's when she heard it.

Not the sound of Climora's snoring, nor an animal sniff-ing about outside... not even voices from surrounding cabins or someone walking by.

It was a scratching sound, *exactly* the sound her char-coal made as she plied it on parchment. And it came from somewhere in this very room.

Her hands trembled as she lowered them from her eyes. Her lids fluttered open and her gaze quickly scanned the room.

Nothing.

No other living soul claimed an inch of space in the room with her.

Yet the scratching continued.

That's when she looked down.

That's when she jumped to her feet, tumbling her chair backward as she gasped and stepped back, skirts tangling about her legs as she nearly fell over the overturned furniture.

Her eyes—unmoving, unblinking eyes—were pasted to the parchment on the table. Her drawing, the best she had ever created, was... moving.

Katrin closed her eyes, tight and hard. Her fisted hands knuckled them as if to will the delusion from her mind.

You are but overly tired. It is naught more than your overactive imagination.

Katrin breathed deeply as she chided herself. Calmed, she opened her eyes and looked down.

"Eek!" she yelped.

She could not help it, for the drawing still moved—or more correctly, there was movement in the drawing.

Witon's hands moved from flat on the table before him, to the clasped position as she had drawn them. Uganta's ears twitched forward and back as if he moved them to listen more keenly.

Katrin slapped her hands on her face, on her eyes.

The scratching continued. She opened them. The movement continued, too.

Before her legs gave out beneath her, the artist reached out shaking hands and—as if she reached for a poisonous snake—she snatched the parchment, rolling it up and shoving it into the small cupboard where she kept all her drawings.

Chest rising and falling with rapid gasps of breath, she stood in silence, listening.

Even through the wooden door, she heard it.

Katrin ran into the other room, jumped into her bed and pulled her blanket over her ears. She dare hear no more.

* * *

Beneath a Star Tree, the name given to those with the five-pointed leaves, she sat in the comfy crux of its large roots, a perfect groove making a perfect seat, her back resting against the large ochre trunk. Katrin laughed merrily, a light treble like those of the birds perched above her, transfixed by the goings-on in front of her.

As the large stream bordering their camp gurgled its way past, two Humans endeavored, with patience and kindness, to teach the Trolls to fish.

"Toss it first behind you, then quickly forward," Igar instructed. "Snap it forward to get a good launch."

Uganta tried first. His bulky, hairy arms moved ungainly and the string attached to the end of the carved, thin pole swung out, snapping forward with a twang instead, wrapping itself wildly about his head, a comical hat atop a chagrined face.

"G… good try," Igar muttered, swallowing his laughter for the sake of the Troll's pride.

"I think I need a larger pole," Uganta chuckled self-effacingly.

"I think—"

Sploosh!!!

The slosh of something large meeting water held Igar's tongue.

Turatan fared far worse than his brother. Ungraceful by nature, he tripped as he made his way into the water and his pole came loose from his hand, floating downstream.

"Hah!" Uganta guffawed. "At least I can walk."

Resetting his pole and string, baiting the small hook on the end, he tried again, and again, and again. As Turatan conquered how to move in water, his brother conquered the movements of the fishing line. The scene enchanted Katrin. But not until Uganta captured a fish, a large, deep indigo fish, did she feel compelled to act.

"Huzzah, huzzah!" Uganta stood in the middle of the stream, fish in one mammoth hand, pole in the other, both raised over his head, arms pumping them up into the sky as he celebrated his own triumph.

Such a precious a moment could not pass unrecorded.

Katrin began to draw.

* * *

"Wake, Katrin, wake."

The small hiss tickled her ear. In her somnolence, Katrin brushed at it, a night thrip unconsciously denied.

"Wake up, Katrin!"

The quiet demand came with a touch, two touches, of two tiny hands gently slapping each side of her face, brushes of feathers. But it was enough.

"Unh." Katrin's eyes fluttered, squeezed tight, then opened to find Climora atop her chest, her wee face mere inches from her own.

The darkness, the dead of night, the frightened look upon the Brownie's face… Katrin awoke in a flash.

Sitting up abruptly, Katrin tumbled Climora onto her lap then held out her open palm for the sprite to climb upon.

"What is it, Climora? Is something wrong?" she asked.

"Shush!" Climora demanded. She smacked her hands upon Katrin's lips, a feeble attempt at closing them.

Katrin raised her shoulders to her ears, eyes bulging in silent demand.

"I th-think," Climora stuttered, not loosening her grip, "I think there's someone... or something... in the other room. Listen!"

Listen Katrin did and it took but a moment to hear it. The scratching had returned.

"Oh, Great Stars, not again!" Katrin tossed the linens from her with her free hand, jumped up, and made for the door, with Climora still perched on her palm.

"Again? What do you mean, again?" Climora demanded, but her question remained unanswered.

In the main room of their small cabin, Katrin placed Climora on the table, turned, and opened the cupboard of her drawings.

The scratching grew louder.

Reaching in, Katrin grabbed the drawing she had made that day, that of the Men and the Trolls fishing.

She held the rolled parchment in her hands, looking down at it, a deep furrow plowing between her brows, her lips pinched in a thin line.

"What... what is it?" Climora asked, her voice a soft tremble. "Does the sound come from... from there?" Her small hand pointed to the roll in Katrin's hand.

The artist looked at her friend and housemate, her gaze roving over the tiny features, a face that had become so dear to her.

With a nod, Katrin told her all; of the scratching first heard but two nights ago, of the movements on the parchment that caused the sound.

Climora paled with every word, a mighty occurrence for such a ruddy-skinned being.

"And you think it is happening again?"

Again, Katrin simply nodded.

"Show me," Climora asked.

Katrin did. Laying the roll upon the table, she unfurled it and swiftly stepped back.

There! There they were. The movement this time encompassed much more... Uganta pumping his arms up in triumph, the Men applauding his catch, his brother pinwheeling in the water, leaves swaying, birds flying.

The picture was alive.

"Great Stars above!" Climora gasped. She walked about the sketch, noting every detail, every movement.

"How... how did you do this?"

Katrin said naught for she had nothing to say. Once more, she raised her shoulders to her ears and stretched out her hands in a hopeless gesture.

Climora stared at her, but only for a second.

"Get thee a clean parchment and your coal."

"W… why d—"

"A test, Katrin," Climora urged, "a test."

Comprehension dawning, Katrin did as urged. Moving aside the fishing scene, she placed the blank parchment before her and sat with charcoal in hand.

Climora struck a pose before her, then started to move. She held up a tiny hand, held it up high, and waved it back and forth over her head while she lifted one foot, then the next, in a constant march.

"Draw me," she urged, "draw me, quickly."

Katrin did.

It took her but a few minutes to complete the drawing, even given the few seconds she allowed herself here and there to grin in delight at her friend's bizarre dance.

Making one last mark, Katrin tossed the nub of coal left in her hand upon the table and leaned back against her chair.

Climora dropped her arm as if dropping a heavy load, stilled her legs and gave them a shake.

"It is done?"

"'Tis."

Moving swiftly, Climora came to stand directly in front of Katrin, nestled in the cove formed by the artist's two arms now resting on the table. Together, they stared at the sketch.

But not for long.

Within minutes it began. First, the drawn arm, then soon the legs followed. Even Climora's long hair joined in, gently swaying to and fro behind her back as the force of the sprite's movement swung in pendulum style.

"You must tell…" the words, when they came, were of the softest command, "… you must tell the king."

Katrin pushed back her chair, its wooden legs screeching against the plank flooring.

"No, no. What if…?"

Climora spun round, eyes narrowed, head tilted and hands on hips. "You have nothing to fear from Witon, ever, and you know 'tis true. "But you must… *must* tell him."

Katrin opened her mouth as if to argue. No words came. Instead, she closed it decidedly and nodded.

"Just let me clean my hands," she said.

Reaching into her cupboard, she pulled out a splotched linen cloth, using it, as she always did, to wipe the soot from her hands. She rubbed… and rubbed some more. All came away save for a very small spot in the wing of skin betwixt thumb and forefinger.

"What is wrong, Katrin?"

Katrin shook her head and turned to the Brownie, hand outstretched.

"This."

She held her hand inches from the Brownie's eyes, but still, Climora stepped closer, leaned down, and squinted her eyes, staring at the mark no larger than a freckle, a freckle Katrin had never had before. When she looked up, her eyes were wide and unblinking.

"It looks like…" Climora shook her head, "… it is a Star."

Katrin brought her hand close to her own eyes, seeing the shape distinctly herself.

Climora said not another word. She jumped off the table to the chair, to the floor and toward the door.

"We go to the king, now."

On shaking legs, Katrin followed.

* * *

The king did not open the door, his brother did. Clad in a nightshirt, his brown hair a tousled mess, his eyes barely open, Mitren stood in the dark threshold and peered into the night.

"Who goes there? What does thee want at such an hour?"

"We are so very sorry, dear Mitren," Climora said, surprising the Man by speaking from the palm of Katrin's hand, "but we must speak with your brother. We must speak with the king."

That word, one that had become a defining one for the family of Lahkrok, worked its magic; Mitren awoke fully, attuned now to the urgency of the moment.

"Come," he said, leaving the door open for them to follow him as he hurried away and into the adjoining room of the cabin, one much like the one Katrin and Climora shared.

Having closed the door behind them, the two nervous creatures stood just inside the room, becoming ever more anxious at the sound of the mutterings in the bedchamber that grew ever more intense. Within seconds of its ceasing, Witon appeared in the main chamber, a look of worry and concern upon his sleep-swollen face.

"My ladies…" He swept them a quick bow, ever the gallant, even in such a moment. "What brings you here? Is something amiss? Are you both well?" The battery of questions obviously sprung from concern, not anger. It helped.

It was Katrin's story to tell and she stepped up to tell it, all of it, pulling out the three parchments and spreading them on the table and a chair and even the floor, so that all could be displayed as one. As she spoke, the brothers Lahkrok walked about them, studying each with narrow-eyed intensity; penetrating gazes flitting between the moving drawings and Katrin's face.

Her tale seemingly told, Katrin fell into silence, loud though it was.

"Your hand, Katrin," Climora whispered but, in the quiet, those three words reverberated like an announcement.

Witon stepped toward the artist, putting his own hand out to her, palm up and open, but his eyes never left Katrin's. In them, she saw no judgment, no condemnation. She saw what should be seen in a king, safety. She placed her hand in his.

Witon raised it, peering at it, even as Mitren came to stand beside him.

"Is that… a… Star?" he mumbled, full of confusion.

"Indeed it is." Climora answered for the tongue-tied Katrin.

Witon raised his gaze to her face, lifted her hand and kissed it, kissed the Star that now branded the artist's hand.

Then he turned and walked back into the other room.

"What… what is he doing…? What have I done?" Katrin asked.

Climora sat in her palm, words failing her. Mitren remained by her side, inching a bit closer as he placed a calming hand on her arm.

"Worry not, fair lady. My brother may have ways we do not understand, but there is always a good and purposeful reason for it. He is just—"

At that moment, Witon returned, but he did not come empty-handed.

He held a stack of papers; held them reverently, as if they were the Great Messages that had been delivered from the Stars thousands of years ago, messages that were stored in the grand vault on Minra Erna, but which had been copied hundreds of times and read thousands more.

The king stood before her and held out the scraps to her.

Four folded sheaves he delivered to her, taking Climora upon his own palm so that Katrin could open and look upon them.

She gasped at what she found. She knew them immediately. They were the four maps of their new kingdom, the original that had been given to Witon by those who had discovered the land and the three that had been sketched by the crewmen who had scouted the land upon their shipwreck. Katrin well knew what they meant to Witon. She looked up at him with wonder and with a silent question.

"Draw, Katrin," Witon said, his voice a quaver of magical possibilities. "Draw them well."

Chapter XX

GIVING AND GIFTS

"I would never have thought it," Mitren mumbled to his brother, as they sat side by side before their cabin on a bench made of the softest, dark blue wood, the strangest wood either had ever seen. It seemed as if it grew for the sole purpose of becoming furniture, it was such a delight to sit upon, as if it cradled one in a loving hand.

The brothers often spent idle time upon the tender perch, catching each other up on their activities and accomplishments, sharing memories only they two could call theirs. And often, more and more often, the same sounds greeted them. The sounds of passionate lovemaking.

"You never would have thought what?" Witon asked, continuing to whittle on the piece of whitest birch which was slowly taking on the form of a bird. Little did he know that the strokes of his knife now moved in time to the sexual rhythm, to the creaking of a wooden cot, to the low, abandoned groans, emanating from two huts down the path.

"That she... that Katrin..." Mitren muttered.

Witon looked up, stared at his brother. He could see the tangle of Mitren's words, his thoughts, on Mitren's face. "That Katrin...?"

Mitren jumped up. "Well, normally she is so... so quiet."

"Hah!" Witon guffawed. "And you assume that a woman who is quiet in public is so in private as well!"

"Well..." Mitren blushed. Witon enjoyed his discomfort immensely. "Well, yes."

Witon laughed harder. "Oh brother, you do have much to learn."

Mitren kicked at a pebble, as he would if he were a two-year-old denied a toy. "Yes, well, there is no one here to teach me, is there?" He looked down the row at the cabin from which the glorious sounds emanated. "Not anymore now."

As if on cue, the moans grew louder, faster, until they erupted, two voices, two bodies, together in bliss.

"Who is it? Do you know?" Mitren turned to his brother, hands splayed on hips in a demanding pose.

Turning back to his whittling, more to hide his grin than to further his work, Witon shrugged. "Lusby, I think."

Mitren threw his hands up into the air. "Of course. Damn those Ghosts."

From the other side of the cabin, in the direction of the meal hall and the large courtyard before it, other sounds reached them, exuberant voices raised in frivolity.

"After what she has been through, what she has achieved, I believe she is well deserving of such satisfaction," Witon spoke with the wisdom of the king he had started to become. "Have you seen it? Is it not the most extraordinary thing you've ever beheld?"

Despite feeling downtrodden by his unrequited love, Mitren could but nod. "It is wondrous indeed, brother. More and more every day it comes to life."

He looked up at his brother. In the depths of Mitren's brown eyes, there shone wonder as well as regret. "She is a magical being now, isn't she?"

Witon simply nodded, a soft smile for the tinge of disappointment he recognized. "She is—and therefore she is ours to protect and all the more for it."

Once again, Mitren could only nod.

Witon stood and clasped a hand on his brother's shoulder.

"They will come. More women will come." He soothed Mitren, much as he did when they were children and his brother woke frightened from a bad dream. "And then you will have your choice."

Mitren looked up into his brother's face. His own scrunched features eased; his lips relaxed, curled ever so slightly.

"Too right," Mitren agreed. "I am, after all, the king's brother. Who wouldn't want to bed me?"

Witon threw back his head and his laughter flew into the air.

"Exactly!" He punched his brother playfully on the arm. "For now, let us join the others. I believe there is a game of flasion taking place. Let's go play."

Mitren needed no prodding to head off before more sounds of lovemaking began.

* * *

With great cheers and greetings, the two brothers were eagerly enfolded into the game, one to a team.

In the large open space before the dining hall, the Men had set up the field. In the shape of a heptagram, six of the points were punctuated by six holes in the ground and at the seventh point, a man stood, a long, flat piece of smooth timber in his hands.

The remainder of the two teams were scattered about the field, some taking an offensive position, while others defended the space before the holes. In the center of the circle, one Man stood, holding in his hands a rather odd, ball-shaped device, made out of the hide of some animal whose flesh had, no doubt, once been their meal. Unlike the krondels on Minra Enra, this one felt somewhat soft, pliable to the touch, rather than the hard ones that were fashioned with such precision out of hide and wood. Nonetheless, it served.

"Are you ready, Pretray?" the Man with the krondel called to the Man with the wood.

"I'm ready when you are, Natrick," the hitter called to his own teammate, the tosser.

"Make it good," Witon shouted, inching closer to his brother who guarded one of the six holes.

If all went well, Natrick would toss the krondel perfectly to Natrick. Natrick would hit the krondel with such precision, it would easily be caught by a member of their team.

It would be that member's duty to charge toward a hole and get it in, by whatever means possible, scoring a point. Most often the means were rough, as the opposing team could grapple and restrain the player with the krondel as much as they wanted to prevent him from scoring. It was brutal and exhilarating; it was the most popular game among Men on Minra Enra, one of the few traditions the pilgrims were happy to continue here in their new world.

Pratrey began to wind his arm, began to trot closer to Natrick, lifting his arm, ready to launch the krondel… when the thunder began; thunder so loud, he dropped the ball to cover his ears.

* * *

She had set off just after mid-day, needing to work her still healing leg, to bring it back to its former strength and power. At least that's what Chalene told herself.

In truth, she needed no one's company but her own and she needed the exertion of a long, hard gallop to bring peace into her mind.

Back in the settlement, she had found no one to talk to, to speak of things from within. Oh yes, there were other females, but what did a Centaur have in common with a Dwarf or a Faerie or a Human? While there was much that all females shared, they could never understand her need for physical exertion, to release and control the power inherent within a body such as hers.

Having let her brother know that she made for the forest—*their* forest, or so she hoped it would become one day soon—Chalene set out under the warmth of the sun. Soon, blessedly soon, her heart pounded and her human arms pumped by her side, as her horse legs careened upon the earth.

Crossing one of the makeshift bridges crossing the small streams gurgling through the land mass, she reached the plains, the mammoth flat lands that stretched out between the settlement and the tall trees of the forest she and Chiron had claimed for the Centaurs, should they ever arrive. Chalene grunted at herself; *when they arrive*, she corrected her thoughts. Correct though she may feel, her mind still wandered to the dark place where no one ever arrived. She was so intent on these thoughts and on the forest she aimed for, she did not see them when they rose up before her.

Chalene reared up on her hind legs with a whinnied screech, dropping forelegs back to earth with a hard thump. Yet still, she could not move.

The whirl of leaves, an ordinary sight on a breezy day such as this, had become more, so much more.

The movement became deliberate, not just a merry a toss by the wind here and there. Chalene stared in wonder as they appeared to dance before her eyes. Dark green leaves of six points, they whirled and twirled about each other, coalescing more and more, become a shape, a single shape, a head.

"Welcome, Chalene."

The mouth of leaves moved, spoke her name. Awed, astounded, Chalene took a few steps backward nonetheless.

"Be not afraid," the voice of the leaves assured her. "We've been waiting for you. They've been waiting for you."

"They...?" Chalene's head tilted far right; her eyes narrowed not only at the strange 'creature'—if that's what it was—before her, but at its words. "Who are th—"

That's when she heard it. The sound of thunder under a cloudless sky. But she knew the sound for what it really was. For a moment, Chalene thought it a herd of her own kind; for a moment, she allowed her desperate desire to rule her mind. But, as the creatures crested the small rise before her, their truth revealed itself.

One of the largest harrases of horses she had ever seen hurdled the rolling hill; there had to be hundreds of them, beauties all, with gleaming coats in every shade from light russet to the blackest black; some with short manes, others with manes so long, they reached out and up into the air in undulating waves.

Chalene pranced about, tossing her head, jumping onto her back legs and pounding the ground with her front hooves. The horse in her felt utter joy as the magnificent herd approached. She whinnied and they answered, the sound loud and boisterous and magnificent.

The face of leaves smiled. "They are so happy to see you as well, Chalene. They have been wild for far too long. You will control them now. They are for you and yours to use, but you must do so with great respect, for they are a wondrous and powerful creature."

"For... *me?*" Chalene's deep, feminine voice squeaked. "Why... why me?

"You know them, as you know yourself. And your heart is true. There could be no one better."

For a moment, Chalene could do or say naught, even as the team approached and surrounded her, as they neighed and nudged her affectionately with their long noses.

"But I—"

Before she could protest, the leaves began to swirl once more. This time, they swirled apart, scattered and became, once again, nothing more than leaves.

Chalene stood in the middle of the mammoth pack; stood and slowly turned in a circle as she looked upon the faces of all these magnificent creatures. Once more, she knew purpose.

Making her way through the throng, she came out at the southern edge of the massive group of animals. Rising high on her hind legs, she whirled her front ones in the air, threw back her head and neighed from the deepest part of her voice. It rang across the plains. Dropping back, she galloped hard, the pack close behind.

* * *

Every Man stopped at the sound; more than a few drew swords. Their game forgotten, the Men on the field, and those rushing out of cabins as the sound grew louder and louder, twirled about, searching up and down for its source.

"What in the name of all the Great Stars…?" one voice said, loudly enough to be heard over the booming sound which grew louder and louder, closer and closer.

Tingling with alertness, Witon walked toward where the sound seemed to be coming from, the path leading out of the settlement, across First Bridge, and into the plains lands.

Just as quickly, he ran back.

"Look out!" he yelled at the men behind him.

"No!" cried Mitren. "Wait! It is Chalene."

"Chalene? What?" Witon spun back round, mouth gaping at the sight.

From along the river bank, they came, with Chalene at the lead, just as Mitren had said. They entered the courtyard and filled it, overflowing onto the four paths that led into it.

"Horses! Horses!" The cry rang out, from Man after Man.

As gently as puppies, the splendid creatures slowed, then stopped. They nuzzled against all the creatures of the settlement who had come out and who eagerly stroked their beautiful manes, their powerful flanks.

Chalene trotted around the circumference of the courtyard, corralling the horses together as best she could by herself. As she passed him, Witon reached out.

"Chalene, Chalene, where did you find them?" he called, above the din of every creature talking at once and horses snorting and neighing.

The Centaur held still, never so beautiful as in this moment, her long hair as wild as the gleam in her pale eyes. She tossed back her head and laughed.

"I didn't find them, they were a gift."

Witon balked, eyes bulging. "A gift to whom?"

"To us, Witon, to us!" Chalene cried.

"But who gave us such a gift."

Spreading her muscular arms wide, she pranced about in a circle.

"This land, Witon, our land!"

Chapter XXI

WHERE WAITING TAKES THEM

The sun shone brightly on a dreary and dismal world; at least that was how Witon saw it. He saw little of the lush greenness of his new home, or the mosaic of bright-colored blooms dotting the landscape into a masterpiece. He knew only the passing of sameness, of days without end, of days without Belamay.

He sat before his cabin, one he now inhabited alone. His brother and a few of the other men had struck out to explore and possibly settle the flatlands flowing from the eastern branch of the surrounding river; a land whose dark earth held the promise of fertility, whose endless plane tempted to be easily plowed.

Mitren's eyes had sparkled when he told Witon of it, of its possibilities. Witon would have kept him close if he could, but he knew the close confines of their small camp were not to the quiet Mitren's likings. Wide, open spaces and a place to forge deep roots were Mitren's wish. As brother and as king, Witon had bestowed both upon

Mitren, though he could not bring himself to smile when doing so.

Dropping his elbows on his knees and his head into his hand, Witon created a sculpture of woe. He remained in this state even as he inhaled the freshest air he had ever known... as the aroma of blossoms wafted in a breeze softly soothing his ruddy skin... as murmurs of friendly voices and even a laugh or two reached him from the gathering of idle creatures not too far down the path, one growing wider with each step upon it.

But their talk and their mirth could not fool him. Witon knew every man and creature worried as much as he; he saw it in their eyes and heard it in their quick, nervous laughter. He could almost sense their very thoughts, knowing they were exactly like his own.

Were they coming?

And worse, though it was astounding to think there could be a more terrible thought, but...

What if they never come?

In moments of rational thought, Witon knew they would be found eventually; explorers had come to this land before, so no doubt they would come again. It was not unfathomable to think that Belamay would launch her own search when too much time had passed without word, or the ship's return.

"Great Stars!" Witon exclaimed, snapping his head up and banging his fists on the bench that sat in front of his cabin.

"Oh dear, does the king blaspheme?"

The tiny voice, thick with more than a hint of amusement, found him and, with a glance outward, Witon saw Vishena once more perched on the back of the majestic Chiron, a sight becoming a more and more common one about camp. How he could not have noticed a Faerie riding on the back of a Centaur down the main path through a settlement as strange as any elder's tale, running straight before his perch, told Witon he had fallen too far into his own dire thoughts.

Heaving a sigh, he nodded. "I fear I have," Witon said with a shake of his shaggy head. He had never let anyone but Belamay cut his hair, and he wouldn't do so now. It had grown as wild as the land and long past his shoulders.

He rose and walked toward his friends; he had no need for Council members in this moment.

As he stood beside them, dwarfed by the enormity of the Centaur looming over the wee form of the Faerie, Witon felt little need to hide his angst.

"The waiting eats at me," he mumbled, kicking the dirt beneath his feet with the worn tip of his boot.

"I'm sorry I cannot be more encouraging," Vishena replied softly. At the last Council meeting, both she and Lydan had reported that while they both *felt* as if they had made true contact, neither could *see* for certain, and no clear message had manifested itself. "But I can tell you my hope is true."

Witon smiled crookedly at the tenacity of the Faerie Queen; in her small, brilliant blue eyes, he saw the truth of her staunch belief. He nodded, accepting her succor yet again.

"In my heart, dear Vishena, so is mine, but this waiting…" he stepped back, flung out his arm as if to speak to the trees, the sky, the very air around them, "…it suffocates me. I… I…"

"You need to get away." Chiron's deep voice cut Witon's whining off as with the swing of an ax. Vishena clapped her hands as Witon's brows rose on furrowing skin.

"Beg pardon?" Witon croaked. Did dissent scuttle among the ranks already? And did Vishena agree with Chiron's notion?

"How marvelously smart of you, Chiron." Vishena gave the large creature a pat on his brawny back and the hide flinched as if pestered by a fly. "We have the solution, dear Witon. You will come with us."

"With… you…?" Witon's curious gaze flit to and fro. "You are leaving, too?"

"Not leaving," Chiron grunted, "merely traveling. You are not alone in your eagerness for the others to arrive. My wife, my children…"

This time, the large creature's bass tones faded to sour notes. Witon's lips thinned into a tight line; how could he be so selfish as not to think others worried as much as he did… that they, too, would be missing family members who had been meant to arrive no more than a few days after they had.

He dared raise a hand up to squeeze the Centaur's shoulder. The gesture spoke of their shared longing; no words could say it as well.

With a nod and the passing of tenderness across his hard features, Chiron continued: "So, we thought a bit of travel, some exploration would do us good."

"Yes, indeed," Vishena chirped. "I was just asking Chiron if he would join me on a trip. I long to show off the land where the Faeries will make their home. I fly there often, but beauty unshared is not nearly as beautiful."

"And I eagerly accepted the invitation."

"As do I!"

Thus came the shout of glee, like that of a child who found a lost toy. It attracted more than one curious gaze from those gathered not far off; to hear their leader joyful was a gift to all.

Witon curled his shoulders up to his ears in embarrassment but soon shrugged it off.

"I would relish the chance to get away, for a change of scenery," Witon said with a modicum of decorum, though his leg twitched, already eager to be underway.

"In turn, I thought to show Vishena the Centaur Forest," Chiron explained, speaking of the land bequeathed by the Council to the Centaur species. "It is nearly straight across the river, I believe. Doing so will lengthen the journey."

"All the better." Witon rubbed his hands together. "As the... well, as I am... ahem, a..."

Vishena laughed, head thrown back, auburn hair sparking in the light. "You are king, Witon. Say it, and be proud."

Witon shook his head with a small chuckle. Vishena claimed she could not read minds; he often didn't believe her.

Straightening his shoulders, standing tall, he tried once more. "As the k-king, it is well for me to peruse the kingdom, to know where all our great creatures shall make their homes. I shall leave Nevod and Lydan in charge of the settlement."

"And I will instruct Flerial to fly to us with great speed should the others arrive in our absence."

For a moment, Witon almost changed his mind. To have Belamay arrive when he wasn't there to greet her was a thought that brought pain to his gut. But the pain of the waiting stung far more sharply.

"Would you welcome Yerten and the Ghosts to the party?" Witon asked. "Yerten is truly amazing with his map-making. I long for his work on the one of our land to continue, and then for him to give it to Katrin, for her to breathe life into it. And Miltra and Lusby could find their way out of the thickest forest in the middle of a blizzard."

"By all means," Vishena agreed. "And the Ghosts are so very interesting to look at."

Chiron grumbled a laugh and the tiny sprite bobbled on his bouncing back. Her love of beautiful men never failed to amuse.

"I think it only ever snows in the mountains, Your Majesty," Chiron said, with little guile.

Witon laughed but shook his head. "Please, my friends, my fellow Council members, to you I must remain Witon."

The two creatures before him shared a look, one he didn't see in the throes of his excitement about the journey.

"When do we leave?"

"At first light on the day after next? That should give all enough time to prepare, don't you think?"

"Plenty of time," Witon replied to Vishena. *Too much*, he thought, knowing he would chew on thoughts of the next ship the whole while. But he scampered off, back toward his cabin, thinking of his rucksack and what he should put in it. "I will see you then, my good friends. And thank you, thank you so very much." He waved as he walked toward his door.

"Our pleasure, Your Highness!" Vishena twittered.

Witon spun back, chiding on the tip of his tongue. But, at the sight of the two creatures, one so small clutching the hair of the one so large as they galloped away, their faces glowing bright with amusement and their lips gaping with laughter, he could only shake his head, give a small laugh of his own and wave once more.

* * *

They crossed the river at the makeshift bridge Mitren and his band of men had created—at least, the Humans of the party did. Chiron waded through, the mild rapids no match for his powerful horse legs. Vishena flew across, hovering on the other side, waiting.

Already, on the far bank were signs of Mitren's work; paths led away from the bridge in two directions, one eastward and one turning north.

"Mitren has suggested this land would make for a fine Human town," Witon told the party, as he walked behind Yerten, steering the map-maker while he scribbled furiously on his parchment, so intent on his work that his step was not always sure. "He has said it has a natural port, just a bit to the north."

North they turned, on the path leading the way and soon they heard the rhythmic sound of ocean and land coming together. They stepped off the path to follow the beckoning sound. Their divergence was well rewarded.

The small group stood at the middle point of the almost perfectly round cove, high up on the white cliffs rising above it and the pale pink beach decorating it from one side of its smiling mouth to the other. From each of these points, as on their perch, lush shrubbery and flowering trees gave a coat of brilliance to the already breathtaking sight. The circular pool of water narrowed to a river; even from their inland position, the group could see open ocean at its other end. Yerten's scratching grew ever more intense.

"Each side of the river's mouth would make the perfect place for dockage," Chiron said, pointing first to one side, then the other.

Witon nodded. "Indeed. From the size of the waves, it appears as if no dredging would be necessary. A Star-send, if true."

"And this would make for a fine retreat," Vishena added. "Such beauty is meant for lovers' eyes."

Witon turned from the amazing vista, only to lay glance upon another, a meadow stretching to the limits of his sight, waving at him as the grasses and wildflowers undulated in the breeze. "I think this whole land was made for those who long for love... love and peace."

It reminded him, reminded them all, that their hardships had not been for naught; not yet, at least.

"Come, my friends." Vishena clapped her tiny hands. "We've a ways to go."

With a last look and a final deep inhalation of the briny scent of the sea, the group made their way back to the path, one not so ingrained as that which ran through camp, being barely discernable through the wild undergrowth, but one the Ghosts found with ease.

"Will we reach your land by nightfall, M'lady?" Yerten asked Vishena. "I'm trying to get a sense of distance, if ye take my meaning."

"I do, indeed." Vishena buzzed about Yerten's graying head. "I don't think Humans could make the journey from the settlement to Faerie land in one day, no. We will need to find a place to camp for a night. But no more than one, I'm sure."

"Faerie land?" Witon repeated. "Is this the name you have chosen?"

"It does have a certain lovely ring to it, doesn't it?" Vishena smile. "But it is not for me to choose, but for us all."

Men and Centaur nodded, no further explanation required. Faeries were perhaps the most democratic species of them all; they considered themselves One in all things, good and bad, in decision-making as well.

Witon's legs began to ache a bit and he could feel the bite of the sun on the back of his neck, having tied up his hair as the afternoon found its warmest moment. Witon sighed with the pleasure of such pains. His sight beheld so much beauty around him, he found himself swallowing a tear or two. His mind wondered and worked on the possibilities of such a tract of land and it served not only to dispel his fear and anxiety about the arrival of the others, but as a sign that they would come. They had to. Such a place much surely be meant for the peaceful coexistence of the species, the goal that hundreds of myriad creatures had committed themselves to.

"Perhaps you could call it—"

Witon snipped off his words, dropping to a crouch. Before them, at the front of the line, Chiron had snapped a hand up, one that insisted not only on stillness but on silence.

In the void, they all heard it… a rustling of shrubbery and leaves, a snapping of a trodden branch. Witon put his hand upon the earth; he felt it, the vibration of footsteps.

As stealthily as possible, he drew his bow from his shoulder, drew an arrow from its quiver, and notched it, waiting.

That's when he heard the laughter.

"Oh, brother, if thou art trying to hide, you have to do *something* with that hair of yours. 'Tis a beacon of blinding light."

Popping up like a gopher launched from its hole, eyes popping wide, Witon beheld Mitren, no more than twenty steps away.

"Brother!" Dropping forgotten weapons, Witon set off at a run, closing the gap between them. Their hard bodies crashed together and they tumbled to the ground with a peal of childlike laughter. "I have missed you, dear Mitren."

"And I you," Mitren laughed. "Now, get off me, you clod."

Witon tossed back his head and laughed; how good it was to be thus insulted.

"I will, but only if you allow us to spend the night at your camp."

Mitren rolled his eyes and formed a mock frown with his lips. "Oh, very well, if you must."

"We must." Witon leaped up, grabbed his brother by the arm and hauled Mitren to his feet.

"Lead on, brother," Witon commanded.

With a fine bow, one worthy of any high court, Mitren replied, "At your service, Your Majesty."

"Oh, don't you start that as well," Witon chided and before Mitren had a chance to ask, his brother spun him about and gave him a shove.

* * *

Within a click of the Sun, they had reached the camp, which was furnished with makeshift lean-tos and a well, already dug.

The travelers were welcomed by the campers and the first question, asked and woefully answered, was gotten out of the way with painful brevity. Jumping onto a stump, Mitren pointed there—where he envisioned the Town Hall to be built—and spun to a point over there—where he imagined the Town Square and shops to rise up—and eagerly, merrily, he pointed east—where he visualized a grand manor house being built and a vast farm being established. Witon had never seen his brother so animated, so invigorated; this alone made the trip worthwhile.

With a pheasant and a rabbit roasting on the pit, the juices spitting on the fire and sending up sparks of delightful aromas, the large group settled into smaller ones, Chiron and Vishena and the Men of their group mingling with the others, while Witon and Mitren sat off to the side, talking quietly amongst themselves.

"I am surprised there have not been more problems," Witon replied, to his brother's question about conditions back at the main settlement. "There is little work to be done other than hunting, fetching wood for the fire and gathering plants for food and medicines. It's not enough to keep all the Men and Creatures busy. And yet it is an amicable place."

"There is something about the air here," Mitren said, with not a hint of jest in his voice.

Witon's brows knit; he turned to stare intently at his brother.

"What do you mean?"

"I mean…" Mitren shrugged, pushing his own long, shaggy hair, a dirtier blond shade than ever before, off his face. "I mean… well, look. Look at the size of our dinner."

Witon turned to the fire and the animals cooking over it; he had to admit they were the largest of their kind he had ever seen. "But could that not just be because no one has ever been here to hunt them, to weed out the smaller, weaker ones?"

Once more, Mitren shrugged. "Perhaps. But perhaps not."

He turned in his seat and, though dusk lay fully upon them, the vegetation close by could be clearly seen in the light of the flames. "But see those apple trees, there, just behind us?"

Witon turned, quickly spied two saplings, both at least four feet tall, and nodded.

"We planted those."

"We? Who we?" Witon's face open wide only to scrunch quickly in confusion. "You we?"

Mitren laughed. "Yes, *we* planted them. On the second day of our arrival."

"But you have only been gone, what, half a Moon cycle? It cannot be."

"No, it cannot be, but it is." Mitren's golden gaze held firm to his brother's. "And the colors, of everything, they are so… so…"

Witon's brows flicked up his forehead. "Yes, the colors... indescribable if not seen."

"As I say, brother, there is something more, so much more, about this place than meets the eye."

Witon held his breath at Mitren's words. They were not the first of their kind he'd heard; he doubted they would be the last. "It is the land of the Great Stars here on Earth."

Mitren stirred the rich earth at his feet with a stick, and the pungent scent of the nutrients and minerals in the soil assaulted their senses.

Witon took up a stick himself. Settling his head in the crook of his arm, he drew circle after circle in the dirt.

"What's wrong, Witon?"

Witon didn't move and his answer came muffled through his shirt. "Wrong? Why do you ask?"

Mitren leaned a hard shoulder into his brother, jostling him. "I've never known you to be so quiet for so long. The Stars knows how your chatter plagued my childhood."

Witon didn't move, but even with his face half hidden, he knew his brother could see his half smile.

"What if she is... is too injured to come?" The lines he drew grew deeper as he pressed harder on his stick, harder and harder until it snapped. He sat up and turned to face Mitren head-on. "What if, after what... what happened, she no longer wishes to come?"

There, the words were out, the nagging, festering thoughts that kicked him in the stomach and snatched away his sleep. Doubts so deep and profound, he had never spoken them aloud to another soul.

As was his way, Mitren did not answer right away. He had always been the less impetuous of the two, more thoughtful and slower to speak and act. It made for the best of brothers and advisors.

"What you really ask, brother, is... what if she no longer wants you?"

With a moan, Witon dropped his head into the basket of his hands. Mitren cut to the core, a necessary incision. He need not answer the question; Mitren knew the answer.

"I suppose it is possible," Mitren mused, voice flat. Witon puffed cynically without moving. "But doubtful."

Witon dared to peek at him with a sidelong glance.

As if he hadn't seen it, Mitren continued. "We have a woman who took over a large barony when her then-husband died before they had been married for two years. She took it over and helped it thrive, though many a man tried to take it from her, though many a creature tried to stop her."

Witon grunted a sound of agreement.

"We also have a woman, the only one I have ever known, one of the few I've ever heard of, who took to the battlefield. Took to it, and owned it. She led men into battle who looked to her as the first Men looked to the Gods. Veteran soldiers who followed her without question. She not only fought, but she fought hard and well."

Witon hummed this time; the sound of his respect and admiration, the like of which he felt for few others than his lady-love.

"And then she gave it all up." Mitren snapped his fingers. "Just like that? And why?"

Witon finally brought his head up. "Because she believed—believed that the peaceful coexistence of the species was the only way to truly live."

"Ah, just so." Mitren returned to his musings. "Belamay does believe. I know she fought for many sides—those who fought to protect what was theirs, never for those who wanted what belonged to others."

It had been the same for Witon. He had never put a life in danger for egotistic, selfish desires, or those who held them.

"But 'tis more than that, Witon. Belamay committed to this enterprise, this new world, for one other reason."

Brother stared at brother for the longest time. The fire crackled, voices murmured and chuckled on the far side of it, and the air sluiced softly through the trees. Witon raised his shoulders in a silent plea.

"For you, Witon. She did it for you."

"But—"

"But nothing," Mitren said with more force than Witon could ever remember hearing from his brother. "Do you really think the woman we just spoke of, the woman who conquered her world against all odds, would allow anything, or anyone, to come between her dreams and the man who lives in them?"

Witon opened his mouth, closed it, opened it again, and then closed it for good.

Mitren laughed, a soft, joyful sound.

"Go to sleep, Witon." Mitren stood, making for his lean-to, grasping his brother by the arm to bring him along. "Your woman, *that* woman, will get here. And the Stars help anyone who dares to stop her."

Chapter XXII

THAT WHICH IS FOUND WITHOUT LOOKING

With a hearty breakfast in their stomachs, many a slap on the back and a long, heartfelt embrace between brothers, the traveling troop left Mitren's camp while the Sun shone with the pale yellow of youth.

"Keep building, dear brother," Witon called, as he turned for one last look at his sibling, one last glance at the small settlement Mitren was constructing. "You are creating a wondrous place here, I just know it."

Without a word, Mitren placed his hand upon his heart—a sign to his brother of his love and tenderness—but once more dropped into a courtly bow, an obeisance to his king, whether the king liked it or not.

Witon turned away with a chuckle.

It didn't take long for the group to find yet another river, no more than a hearty stream in truth, nor did it take long for Yerten to add it to his growing map. On the far side of the flowing water, the mountains rose up sharply before them.

"Are these the mountains Swerin has spoken for?" Witon asked Vishena, as the group stood peering upwards. The massifs were both majestic and frightening at the same time.

"I believe so," Vishena replied. "Of course, the Dwarf King will make the final decision."

Witon nodded, knowing the ways of the Dwarves were not like those of Faeries. The Dwarf world operated as a dictatorship more than a monarchy, and woe to those who dare try to change it. Even in this burgeoning new world, Witon felt sure the ruler would be one who listened to none save himself. Witon hoped he could find the middle ground if he did indeed have a kingdom to rule.

"They would truly serve perfectly." Witon agreed with Swerin's assessment. "But where is your land, Vishena?"

With a whizzing of her wings, Vishena rose higher and higher in the air.

"On the other side," she yelled down to them, a bright smile in her voice.

"Ugh," Yerten groaned, dropping his pack from his back to stow away his parchment and drawing tool. "Mountain hiking. Joyful!"

"You will be joyful, dear Man, when you see what awaits us on the other side. And worry not, it can be done before the sun sets."

Chiron galloped off, leaving the four Men to stare at each other.

Witon shrugged and made the first step. "We've come this far…"

"Too right," Lusby said.

And together, they began the ascent.

* * *

Vishena spoke true and though they were tired and hungry, and more than a little sore, they had made the pass in swift time. The Sun, not yet a day older, still gleamed as they made it to the foot of the mountains on the other side, casting a burnt orange glow upon the world below. The path had been a narrow one, as if sometime, long ago, it had been used before, but now growth on either side dared to obliterate it.

At its aperture, they zigzagged their way through a thin line of trees, and the valley opened up before them like the arms of a loving mother.

"Oh, My Gracious Stars," Yerten whispered. It was a prayer, a discovery of the miraculous.

What they gazed upon held all Vishena had promised... and more.

The hills unfolded gently away from them, here and there dotted by a tree, but trees unlike any they had ever seen. Their seemingly furry leaves curled this way and that, as if they were made of hair and were not leaves at all. And their color was a shade of green unlike anything any of them had seen before.

The crook of the large valley blossomed with a riot of blooms, once again of an unknown type, too beautiful to be real: puffballs of red, sunbursts of purple, ribbon petals of yellow.

"I have never..." began Miltra.

"Nor I..." agreed Lusby.

"You feel it too, don't you?" Vishena whispered, soft echoes of awe in her voice.

Witon nodded his head, unblinking, mouth flapping open like a fish.

They separated, slowly walking in different directions, mindless of destination.

Witon looked at their faces and felt the same expression on his own features. Transfixed, enchanted. They walked only to immerse themselves further in this wondrous place.

They reached the valley floor and, like stars colliding, met in the center of the basin. Here, they stood in a circle, smiling at each other foolishly.

Witon held a hand up before his face, studying it, wiggling the fingers as if they belonged to another's body. "You could not pick a more wondrous place for the Faeries. The energy here... I tingle with it."

Vishena lit on the tips of the fingers he held before him and wrapped her small arms about the largest. She smiled, her glow pulsing with pleasure.

"If there is magic in this great land of ours, and there is, I have no doubt," Chiron intoned, "it emanates from here. Of that, I am sure as well."

"Yes." Witon nodded agreement, his silver eyes round with amazement as he gazed about, up the green hillsides to his left and right, and then down to the long length of the valley. "There is magic everywhere, but here most of all."

Without any discussion—any words—the small group began to make camp, their silence a loud declaration in their desire to simply *be* in this place.

The Ghosts climbed the rolling hills once more, vanishing into the thin width of forest and, within a matter of minutes, they returned with two wild turkeys on the ends of their bows; at least, they looked like turkeys but were as large as a boulder. The juicy birds soon roasted over a spit. As the group settled down to their meal, Vishena told them of her plans.

"I know this is truly where the Faeries belong," she began. "Our realm on Minra Enra was fine, but it was not *our* place. I knew it as truth the first time I came here."

"You and all the Faeries belong here, I feel it," Witon said between bites of his meal, pungent juice running down his fingers as he smiled at her.

"Yes," Vishena chirped. "But I am thinking it needs to be more."

"More?"

"Yes, more than just the village of the Faeries."

Men and Centaur passed round the same confused expression.

"What more would you do?" Lusby finally asked the question in all their minds.

Vishena set her wings into motion, her long auburn hair rising in undulating waves as the air pulsated around her, and she whirled slowly about her fellow travelers, flying a circle around the fire and over their heads.

"Well, as I see from Yerten's map, we are almost at the mid-point of this land."

"An astute observation, Your Highness," Yerten agreed, his pleasure at his map being part of the Faerie Queen's thoughts bursting in pink spots upon his sun-darkened cheeks.

"Thank you, dear Man." Vishena swirled round him. "This land will be passed by all those who travel from North to South and East to West, a central point of sorts. What better place to build an inn? What better than an inn run by the Faeries?"

Her words created a moment of silence, but a very short one.

"Fantastic!" the staid Yerten cried enthusiastically.

"What an absolutely splendid idea!" Witon crowed with delight, forgetting the meal he had been so consumed with consuming. "I know of no better place or of a better species to do so. In all my travels, I have never felt more welcome than in the home of a Faerie."

The Ghosts agreed with quiet fervor.

"We make excuses to cross into their land..." Miltra began.

"Whether we need to or not," Lusby finished with a grin on his pale lips.

Vishena laughed merrily. "So you think my plan a good one?"

"We think your plan a grand one," Witon crowed once more, rising to his feet. "Where would you build it?"

They all stood then as they followed Vishena about, as she flit here and there, outlining the plans for the inn, a structure as large as her dream for it. Each Creature and Man offered ideas and suggestions and they tossed them about the bloom-filled meadow as they would a krondel in a game of flasion.

Vishena stopped suddenly, in the middle of the group, in the center of what would be the main room of the inn, a tear forming in her tiny, glowing eyes.

Witon approached, his steps slow and deliberate. "Vishena? Are you... are you well?"

The tiny sprite laughed in response, the sound like the tinkling of a miniscule bell. "Oh, I am. I am well indeed, dear Witon."

The Faerie darted in a circle, a downward spiral, till she lit upon a large, smooth leaf, one whose edges looked like a row of ruffles upon the finest of gowns.

"The dream of freedom brought me here, a dream the whole of my species longed and prayed for. But this..." she waved a tiny hand to encompass the valley and the inn she could see standing in its cradle one day, "... this is a dream beyond thought, beyond imagination."

Witon squatted beside her, lowering his face so she could see his smile, see the joy he felt for her writ so plainly there. "Our world is not a place where dreams come true, but where dreams are made."

Vishena's lips quivered as their corners turned up. She raised one hand, no bigger than a freckle and placed it tenderly upon his cheek. "All thanks to you, dearest Man."

He shook his head, but just barely, the tender smile never leaving his lips. "Thanks to all of us who believed."

"To all of us," Yerten warbled, his gruff voice overflowing with emotion.

Dabbing her moist cheek, Vishena took to the air once more, heading back toward their campfire. "Folderol and fiddle-dee-dee." Her twittering words, dowsed with laughter, shed their sentiment dispersing into the air in which she flew. "Let us take our rest, my good companions. We shall return to our settlement in the morn. Let us dream of our families awaiting us."

"Ah, a worthy dream." Lusby began to skip toward her, his paleness a fire burning from within, setting him to glowing like the Faerie he followed. Together, the two bright Creatures circled each other, giggling like small children as they headed toward their packs and the fire. Witon could only smile at their joyous abandon, at their dichotomous picture—a fiery Faerie Queen and ghostly grown Man dancing in the darkness of a splendid valley. It became an indelible image from its inception; one he would tell to Katrin, to ask her to record; one he would cherish.

They stoked the fire, unrolled their blankets and, in the warmth of both, lay down to rest.

Witon closed his eyes but thought it would be impossible to sleep. His mind whirled now with possibilities... with the realization of just how great this new world of theirs could be. But the dogged, biting thoughts, the worries for Belamay and the others, nipped constantly at his mind. Would all these wondrous hopes for Witonia—he rolled closed eyes at the name—be just that... unrealized hopes? For, if the others never arrived, they would simply die out, till they were naught more than a mythical tale told to children on Minra Enra, to spark the next generation with thoughts of exploration, or to squash those thoughts before they were fully realized.

Rolling over, he began to count Yerten's snores, an old habit from so many years of trying to find rest on a battlefield. Rather than allow the raucous sounds to annoy him, he used them to pull his mind from truly troublesome topics. Soon, the rhythm began to soothe, until...

Her voice jolted him awake. Witon had jumped to his feet before his eyes had opened fully.

She was here, she was here!

The words were on the tip of his tongue, aching to be screamed, but when he looked around, those nearby still lay deeply bound by slumber.

Witon looked back up and Belamay had taken a step from him, a step away.

He could not let her go.

That creamy skin he so longed to stroke glowed in the darkness. She pursed her full lips and held one finger before them, as if in a kiss. But it was meant to keep him silent. Witon smiled; she wanted their reunion to be a private one. He had no problem with the notion... none at all. Her other hand beckoned to him, urging him ever forward, towards her, even as she slowly stepped backward, away from the campsite.

How did you get here? When did you get here?

Witon longed to scream his questions at her, to explode with the happiness that coursed through his body and mind at the sight of his beloved. Her raven hair danced in gusts of wind, the same winds that wrapped her thin linen gown so tightly to her curvaceous body; her hips swayed as if with the rhythm of intercourse; her magnificent breasts bobbled ever so slightly, ever so tantalizingly, as her nipples strained against the taut, thin material.

Though the Moon slept and the valley lay blanketed in darkness, Witon knew where he walked. He sensed that Belamay urged him westward, along the length of the valley. He trod forward without hesitation, knowing, remembering that there was naught in the space between them that could harm him. Nothing could come between them again, not after all this time, all this heartache.

Belamay quickened her step, almost running from him. Witon hurried to catch up. His heart slammed against his chest, his breath came faster and faster at the thought of her in his arms, and his smiled slashed brilliance across his animated features.

Only a few steps away from him now, his lover stopped and turned and held her arms out and open, a hallowed space for him to fill.

Witon reached out his arms for her.

He took the last step toward her.

And blackness engulfed him.

Chapter XXIII

FRIEND, FOE, OR FIEND

It was ground that he woke upon, yet it was unlike any earth or dirt he had ever known.

Sluggishly, Witon flattened his hands beneath his chest and pushed. The ground felt as if it would give way beneath him, as if he lay on the softest, thickest mattress and not ground at all. But the crumbly feel and deep earthy smell told him its truth.

Sitting up, Witon squinted into the darkness surrounding him. Turning his head as far as he could, first one way and then the other, he found no light. And yet there *was* some in this strange place.

He looked up.

Many, many feet above his head, a circle cut a hole in the ground above him, a hole that had snatched him cleanly out of the valley. Through it, the gray light of a coming dawn or a rainy day floated towards him, too weak to engulf the entire space he now occupied. Even if he stood on tip-toe and reached his long arms upward, he would never reach the oculus and the freedom it taunted him with.

Witon rose to his knees with a sudden thought; if he had fallen into this place following Belamay, where was she? Had she ever been there in reality, or only in his dreams? He sighed deeply, harshly.

He knew the very air of this place—this world—was different, as if filled with a glowing dust. And yet he could breathe it perfectly. It was silent and yet it wasn't. There was a hum, or was it a buzz? He could hear, yet couldn't; know it, but not name it. It filled him with... joy. As it drew closer, as it grew louder, he felt something else. Something he had not felt since the moment he had awoken on the shore and found himself in this strange land. As the buzz became a high-pitched trill, Witon felt fear.

* * *

"He would not have just *left*," Lusby thundered, stomping about as if doing so would bring Witon out from hiding, though there appeared nowhere for him to hide.

As soon as the entire party had woken, as soon as they had seen Witon's empty bedroll, the searching had begun. Vishena flew from one end of the valley to the other, a zigzag flight encompassing the whole of the basin floor. The Ghosts had made for the woods on the south cliff-side, while Yerten climbed the hills to the north. All had returned more fearful than when they had departed.

"Even if he had decided to return without us..." Miltra began.

"... why would he leave all his belongings behind?" Lusby finished.

"He wouldn't *just leave*," Yerten grumbled, "no matter what—"

"Please, dear Men," Vishena zipped about their heads like an angry bee, "you must give me quiet. You must let me *look*."

The three Men immediately did her bidding, knowing she looked with her particular brand of sight.

* * *

They surrounded Witon before he knew what—or who—was upon him. He stood up as they encircled him, crouching slightly, hands forming fists with instinctual defense. But it seemed all for naught.

They were no more than diminutive flying creatures, as shaped and elusive as wisps of smoke, ones no larger than his shortest finger. They seemed to possess neither arms nor legs as each end of their being came to a point, and yet they hovered about him with seemingly no physical effort, as if they floated, not flew.

Witon longed to reach out and touch them but knew instinctively that he could not, should not. So he did what seemed natural; he knelt before them.

"We are this land's natural inhabitants. You and those with you have violated us and our home. Why?" A hundred voices spoke as one.

Or did they?

Even as many drew ever so close, as they brushed past him, he could see pinpoints of light that may have been the creatures' eyes, but he saw no mouths. Yet he knew he had heard their words.

"I... I... we..." Witon couldn't continue, for he didn't know how he communicated. He would have sworn on the Great Stars that his lips did not move. He raised his shoulders from their slump and embraced what he could not explain. "We came for freedom, to live in peace. Our world, our old realm, was a place of evil and hatred and constant fighting. We who are here wanted no more of it."

"Liar!" one voice, or many of one voice, screamed.

The tiny creatures began to swirl about. They coalesced into one larger, more intent form. Witon fell back unconscious as the form struck his head.

* * *

"I fear we do not have a choice." Vishena could not keep the quiver from her voice. She stood upon the hand of Lusby, the other two Men standing on each side of him. The Faerie Queen looked at the ravaged faces before her and knew hers looked the same. But there was nothing for it. "We must return to the settlement. M-Miltren..." her words tripped on themselves, "the others must be told."

Not one of the Men before her denied her words. Though Miltra shook his head, he did so in silence.

"I will carry his things," Lusby said, as Vishena floated from his hand.

The sun had dawned on the third day without sight or sound of Witon. Even as they packed, Yerten gave voice to what they all prayed.

"He will be there." One gnarled hand wiped at his nose. "We will return and he will be there."

No one answered him.

They battered him and they badgered him, but Witon could not tell them what he knew to be untrue. Even if his honor allowed it, he knew it would bring not only his death, but that of all those who had come with him.

He answered their questions, explained why they were there and what he dreamed this world could be for those he had brought with him. Over and over, he spoke the same words, the same message, no matter what they did to him, how much he ached or how weak he became.

"I did not know," he said, or thought, or said, dropping his shaking head into the basket of his filthy hands. "I swear I did not know the land was already spoken for. If we could leave, I would. I would never take another's land. I would never want to become like those in my world, who would do so without thought or care."

With the same words came the same response. They left him, twirling about themselves and away, leaving him bereft even at their abandonment, so alone had he become.

Witon watched the days pass through the small hole over his head. His mind, his entire being, longed to scream out, to call the names of Vishena, Lusby, and the others, but his mouth would not form the words, his throat would not make the sounds. In his haze of degradation, he knew these creatures had the power to stop him calling for help. He feared and revered them all the more. Witon's mind became obsessed with thoughts of Belamay. He felt certain he would never see her—hold her—ever again.

Witon heard them then, the twitter of Vishena, the grumble of Yerten.

Witon tried to stand, tried to call out once more, but he failed at both.

Witon was lost, and in the abandonment and the abyss, he lost consciousness once more.

* * *

On waking, he looked up, his eyes spinning in his head. The Oculus shone no light. There was nothing above him except a black sky and perhaps a small planetary star or two, not one of those which he worshipped so fervently.

Witon dropped his head back down, his unshaven chin grazing his chest. It had been days uncounted since he had had any more than a sip of water or a crumb of bread, and weakness threatened to overtake him. He searched the ground for a forgotten speck of food.

In that moment, he saw her.

"Belamay! Oh Great Stars, you have brought her to me!" He wept, but cared not. He pushed himself to his knees. The dizziness returned; he couldn't stand.

She stood before him without speaking, her bountiful hair untethered and wild about her glowing face. With her chin dipped, her slanted eyes locked on his, and she began to disrobe. Reaching down, she grabbed a swath of her simple gown's skirt in each hand, and pulled upward, revealing the thinnest of linens beneath.

Witon groaned at what he could see through it, and what he couldn't.

Belamay tossed aside the gown, running her free hands down the length of her body and back upward. At the low scoop neck of her under-gown, one so low it revealed the beautiful mounds of her flesh to the tips of her beige nipples, each hand grabbed a side of the fabric... and ripped. Her chemise tore down the middle... slowly, wrenchingly, until she exposed every bit of herself to him.

Witon couldn't breathe. He knew how hard he was, how badly he ached, yet he couldn't move, couldn't take his eyes from her. She did the work for him.

Her hands languished upon her body. Her long, lithe fingers teased her nipples till they grew taut and pointed. Belamay licked her lips with the pleasure she gave herself. Her eyes fluttered with it.

Witon grew weak; his own hands found his hardness and he pushed against it.

One of Belamay's hands fluttered down the slope of her stomach, moving slower and slower until it passed her dark patch of hair. Witon watched, enraptured, as Belamay's own fingers moved back and forth, then in circles. She gasped lightly, bringing her hand up so he could see the wetness upon it, only to plunge it back in to tease and play even more.

Witon rose to his knees and stroked himself, knowing the pathetic groan came from deep in his own throat.

At the sound of it, she moved closer to him. With one hand still on his own pulsating member, the other reached out for her, stretched for the engorged breasts she now held in both hands, as if she offered them to him on the plate of her fingers, as one finger of each hand teased the nipples, demanding they stay tight and hard for him.

Belamay took the last step, bridging the remaining space between them. With a moan of relief and need, Witon laid his head upon her stomach, felt the smooth flesh beneath his cheek, smelled her…

Wait, stop! his addled mind screamed at him. This wasn't right. Something was not as it should be.

Her smell. Belamay's smell, one of sweetness and muskiness at the same time; he couldn't smell it.

Witon looked up at the face he loved more than his own life, but he knew… he knew then that it was not her. This was them; them, with another of their tests.

As tears coursed down his dirt-streaked cheeks, he put one hand on each of her full hips… and pushed.

"Away with you, demon!" Witon cursed, even as he dropped to the ground once more. "You are not my love and we are not here to hurt. These are truths undeniable and nothing you can say or do to me will change it."

The creature 'Belamay' shattered and scattered into thousands of those who held him captive. They swirled and whirled about themselves, till another shape formed, one of a face; a face much like his own.

The 'face' opened its lips, offering words he had never dared hope to hear.

"In you, we have found all that is good and true. You have proved yourself. We believe you."

Witon doubled over, covering his face with his hands, unable to speak.

"It has been foretold that One would come and bring glory to this land. One whose heart knew the true meaning of loyalty and whose strength could defend it."

The buzzing of the creatures rushed at him. Witon sat up, flinched back. The 'face' hovered but an inch from his own.

"W… who are you? Why are you so pale, so white? Are you nothing?" The thoughts hammered loudly in his mind. In the visage before him, he saw hundreds, nay, thousands of the unique, utterly beautiful, wretchedly frightening creatures.

"We are everything. In the one and the many. Our color is in everything." In one voice, they answered, "We are called the Fray."

"The F… Fray." Witon tasted the strange word upon the tongue of his mind. "Where did you—"

But the Fray allowed him no more questions; they questioned instead.

"In time, we will tell you more. When we see in truth that you are as we think." The collective Fray loomed ever closer. "Do you swear upon those of your blood, those who have come before and those yet to come, that you will keep this land a land of peace? That you will keep our existence unknown to any others but the One who will rule after you, and they the One after them, so that we may coexist in peace as well?"

Witon's face crumbled; his shoulders shook with his sobs. He swallowed, longing to speak, not sure if they would allow him to but knowing he must.

"The peaceful coexistence of the species…" he muttered and his tear-swollen eyes popped, for this time he heard his own words; he *could* speak! "I swear it, good Creatures, dear Fray, I swear it with my blood and the blood of all those who I will call mine."

* * *

They had just reached the crest of the southern rise when the sounds reached them.

First, a loud swish, like a gale wind, then a thump, like something hard hitting something just as hard. But the sound that halted Yerten and Vishena, Lusby and Miltra, was the groan. A loud, gasping groan of pain and air forced from a body.

As one, they swiveled back round so fast that Yerten fell, tumbling a few feet back down the hill. He landed in a sitting position at its base, which only allowed him to see better.

"W… Witon!" Yerten rose to his knees and pointed, his head jerking back and forth between the others and the body that had suddenly appeared just a few feet from where they had camped. "It is he!"

Lusby began to run. Miltra quickly followed.

Vishena could but hover where she was, trembling as she did so, and whisper, like an echo, "It is he."

Chapter XXIV

THE END OF...

Witon imagined again, he knew. This time, his musings found him returned to his hut, comfortable and cozy upon the soft ticking of his bed. In the distance, a warming fire crackled, the tantalizing aroma of cooking meat teased him. His thoughts ran wild, he knew.

But such thoughts were kind and, in his half-conscious state, he could almost feel the soft, yet strong hand upon his; he could almost hear her voice calling his name.

"Witon, my love, wake up. Witon? Witon?"

He sucked in his breath and sat up as if stabbed. The hut remained shrouded in darkness and his first fleeting glance told him nothing was out of place, only that his dreams were becoming far too real and the creatures were becoming far too adept in recreating his reality.

Until he felt her lips on his.

Witon pulled back in fright, his mind catching up to actuality in a mere flash of time. He saw her pale face—glowing in the thin moonlight—her dark hair falling around her in waves. He saw her huge, tear-filled eyes and the full, sensuous mouth. He smelled the sweet muskiness of her.

She was there. Somehow, someway, he was safely returned and Belamay—the real Belamay—was there.

"Oh, my love!"

Witon flung his arms about her and pulled her into a crushing embrace. He pushed her from him to gaze once more at her face, but just as swiftly pulled her back into the clinch of his arms.

"I thank ye, oh Great Stars, I thank ye." Witon sobbed as he whispered the words, rocking back and forth as he held Belamay tightly, their tears mingling on their skin as their bodies and hearts tangled together in reunion. "I will keep my promise, and all those of my blood, I swear it."

* * *

With gentle but knowing hands, she straightened his opulent attire. With a snicker, he did the same for her, rubbing his hands over her plump breasts, brushing her nipples with a quick, decadent swipe of his thumbs.

Belamay gave him a half smile, shaking her head at his playfulness. Looking up into his silver eyes, she sobered. "Are you ready, my love?"

Witon sucked in his breath; it rushed from him on a wave of both excitement and anxiety. "I am. Somehow… I am."

Belamay smiled. "You've been ready for this the whole of your life, but you are only just realizing it."

It was Witon's turn to shake his head, to glory at the breadth of this woman's intelligence and insight, at the blessings of the Great Stars that had made her his wife.

"And what of you, my beauty?" Witon turned her round, pressing her back into his chest, crushing the length of his body against hers. "Perhaps we should sneak away and celebrate alone." At the very thought of it, he grew hard and he pressed his growing cock hard against her firm, round ass.

"Behave, little boy, you have a duty before you," Belamay laughed, but not without arching her back and grinding her buttocks firmly against him. Witon closed his eyes at the pleasure of it, one he thought never to know again.

They had been through much, too much, to reach this point. Both their lives had hung in the balance more than once; even in the surety of their love, of their actions, Witon had thought never to see her, feel her, again. It had all but broken him. Yet here they stood, as close as two Humans could be, about to launch upon their greatest adventure yet.

He leaned down close to her, his lips against her ear, feeling her flesh tingle at his touch. "I would have no duty, I would have nothing, without you."

Belamay turned ever so slightly, touching his cheek softly with her hand, and Witon saw the tear in her eye, a rare sight indeed.

At that moment, the low drumbeat began. Her cue.

Belamay took a deep breath, lifted her chin, squared her shoulders and walked through the curtain held open for her.

Though he could not see, the rousing cheer greeting Belamay's appearance told him everything he needed to know.

Witon stood alone now, stood at the apex of the dream that was this new world and of a life within it.

"Oh Great Stars, I thank you for your blessings, for the multitude of your gifts. I swear I will be worthy of them."

Having spoken these words, he nodded to the two young squires holding the curtain closed. At the signal, they opened it for him.

Witon walked slowly down the long path of plush red carpet. Horn players blared a regal tune, growing louder and stronger as though riding the wave of the emotions in the room. The cheers that had welcomed Belamay became a roar at the sight of him.

He longed to look upon every single one of the faces lining the path on each side; to share spiritually the magnitude of the moment—a moment every creature here and upon this land had struggled to achieve. The weight of the gold and purple vestments he wore was but a symbol of the burden he officially undertook this day. At the path's end stood the dais, where Belamay—also attired in gold and purple—waited for him. Her face glowed. Her pale cheeks radiated a bright pinkish blush, blooming with pride in her husband and the warmth of the child growing within her ever-expanding belly.

Witon smiled at the sight of the bulge, knowing it would very soon be ready to burst.

This day had been long in coming. The man who would be king had insisted the coronation should wait until the land and all its creatures were established. Some, those who knew him well, wondered if it was Witon who needed more time to prove—to himself most of all—that he could do it, that he could rule and rule well. In the little more than a year since they had first blundered onto the shores of this land, the bruised and battered stew of creatures had given birth to a nation.

Each species had established their own village and, thanks to remarkable weather and the fecund farmland, the Freedom II had made ten trips to Minra Enra and back, and each time, the cabins overflowed with other pilgrims seeking a land in which to live in peace.

Witonia's Pride, a mammoth six-masted cargo vessel, had completed seven trips of her own, populating the kingdom with cows, sheep, and other necessary livestock not found on this land.

As the population grew, as creatures of one sort took up residence around many others, as they traded and visited with each other with nothing but peaceful intentions, Witon's belief held true: every manner of creature could coexist in peace and freedom.

The very path he walked gave proof to his philosophy and ability to bring dreams to fruition. It was just a stone's-throw from the Castle of Witonia—which as yet consisted of no more than the center keep of a planned three-section castle design— and the very existence of the keep and this amphitheater after such a short time, showed that he could—would—make this land a success.

Carved into a stone so large that a ship could fit into the hole crafted it from it, the amphitheater had been Witon's answer to the unanswerable question of how to remove the mammoth stone which, like everything on Witon, was far grander than any ever seen on Minra Enra. Twenty rows of benches ran round it, leading down to the pedestal, round as well, large enough to hold two center thrones and a semi-circle of eight smaller thrones and two long platforms on each end. Each smaller throne served to seat a member of the Council. The platforms were for the Centaurs. Encircling the entirety of the coliseum, seven towering columns rose up into the violet sky, one for each species that believed in the possibility of this peaceful land. The columns represented each race of Creatures that had gathered their courage and their strength to leave all behind, to make this world and its way of life a reality. Each one was graced with a large, swirling capital, above which was an intricately carved frieze that denoted that particular species in all forms of movement and shapes and sizes.

Witon approached the center set of five steps leading up to round stage and strode to Belamay's side, to take his place before the high-backed purple and gold throne. Together they sat, their hands finding each other's in the small space between the enormous chairs which were carved of purple wood engraved with the symbols of each of the land's founding Creatures… Dwarves and Trolls, Brownies and Faeries, Centaurs and Elves, and Humans.

With the curved back and slow steps indicative of his age, Wolfrin, the oldest Human that had made the migration to Witonia, came forward. Behind him followed the eldest of each species. Between them, they held the wisdom of the ages; who better to crown the land's first King and Queen?

With quivering hands but a strong voice, one loud enough to be heard by the hundreds packing every inch of every bench surrounding them, Wolfrin held up the smaller of the two crowns over Belamay's head.

"Great Woman, do you swear to the Great Stars and all who are here and hear you, to guard this land with your blood and devote yourself to the peaceful Kingdom of Witonia?"

Belamay's throat bobbed on a deep swallow. And then she smiled. "I so swear."

Wolfrin lowered the jeweled crown—one of Swerin's first great creations—upon her head and then, as if he were her father, pinched the apple of her cheek and gave her a wink. Belamay's eyes fluttered and once more grew uncharacteristically moist.

Turning to the gray-haired Dwarf female behind him, Wolfrin picked up the second crown, six-pointed, with sapphires as big as a fist beneath each point, and turned to Witon.

"Great Man," he began once more, his voice ever louder if with a bit of a quiver, "do you swear to the Great Stars and all who are here and hear you, to guard this land with your blood and devote yourself to the peaceful Kingdom of Witonia?"

"I so swear!" Witon cried out, all the joy and churning emotion in his being coming out with a roar. As Wolfrin lowered the crown upon his head, the crowd roared as well, louder than ever.

Witon took Belamay's hand once more, but this time he held their clasped hands up, above their heads, and the assemblage jumped to their feet, their jubilance a monstrous bellow.

Lowering their arms, Witon gave his wife's hand a squeeze, then cleared his throat, preparing to address the audience for the first time. He opened his mouth, only to fall silent.

Something was happening... something he knew nothing about.

The elders had stepped back, bowing as they did so, and had retreated from the dais. But in the same moment, the moment Witon had planned to make his speech, both Lydan and Swerin rose from their thrones, retrieving objects that had thus far lain hidden behind them, and approached the newly-crowned rulers of their land.

Lydan's smooth cheeks held a tint of a pink blush, a strange effect of excitement, as he approached Belamay. Before he spoke a word, Belamay's full lips had already parted, her eyes gaping at what he held in his hands.

It was the slimmest, most finely wrought bow she had ever seen. With the back made of the harder purple wood of the Tribute trees and the belly from the softer, more bendable lemonwood, its colors resembled the official shades of Witonia.

Lydan dropped to one knee and raised the bow, with an embroidered quiver full of arrows, to Belamay. "My dear Queen, the Elvin community, with the help of all the great species of Witonia, pays you tribute with this bow, the Bow of Belamay."

Belamay turned a face sparkling with delight to Witon, who smiled and tipped his head at her, urging her to take it.

Standing in the way only very pregnant Women do, Belamay somehow made it look graceful, reaching down to take the bow, holding it in her hands as she soon would her first child.

"Thank you, sweet Lydan." She raised her voice, clearing it of its tremble of emotion. "Thank you all, good Creatures. No finer gift have I ever received."

As if to prove her gratitude as well as the bow's fineness, she notched an arrow, and aimed the bow—perfectly sized from her knees to the top of her head—upward at a small pigeon that dared to cross the sky above the amphitheater at that very moment. She took aim in a heartbeat. With a sharp, resounded twang, Belamay loosed the arrow. It flew straight and true, piercing the very center of the tiny fowl's belly.

The crowd, still on their feet, roared with approval. The lucky Troll standing in just the right spot, held up the pierced pigeon and the roar grew louder.

"Well done, My Lady," Lydan said, kissing Belamay on each cheek. He went to take the bow from her, but she held fast.

"I only meant to hold it for you," he explained.

"No need," Belamay said, lowering her swollen form back onto her throne and laying the bow across her lap. "I should like to keep it, if you please."

"It pleases me greatly," Lydan said, with another uncharacteristic blush.

Bowing to them both, he stepped back, allowing Swerin to step forward, to step before Witon.

Witon sat up straighter, leaning forward in his large seat, almost quivering with excitement at what he saw in Swerin's hands.

Far longer than Swerin was tall, the leather scabbard boasted the embellishments of the symbols of the Seven Species and seven bands of gold wound their way around it.

Bowing before the newly crowned king, the Dwarf held out the sword, the shining look upon his face one of breathtaking pride.

"To you, our First, our greatest King, we, the inhabitants of Witonia, honor you with this blade. May you only use it if you must, but if you must, may it forever strike sharp and true."

Witon stood, too excited not to, and took the offering with two hands, marveling at the scabbard itself, perhaps for too long.

Belamay stood and, as best she could, reached around her husband, wrapped the leather baldric around his hips and clasped it securely. The sword in its scabbard fell perfectly against his hip and his long leg, its point ending exactly at mid-calf, a long blade indeed.

Witon flicked a smile to his beloved, but quickly shifted his gaze back to the sword. The time had come. His hand reached for the golden grip and the swirl of infinity that swerved as its pommel.

With the *shhhinnng* of profound sharpness, he pulled the steel from its sheath and held it before his eyes.

At the same moment, the earth began to shake, the color of the sky changed from violet to purple, and the glow of the sun changed from pale tangerine to deep, burnished gold.

The crowd gasped in awe and fear, holding onto each other, looking to their rulers on the dais before them.

"Do no—" Witon began, but could not finish, for the noise had begun.

It rose up around them, from the birds, and the animals, from the very trees themselves, a chorus from the Great Stars and their place in the Heavens.

Every Creature looked about them. They saw the animals and birds come out of the trees to take their place around the circular theater; even the trees seemed to edge closer. The Creatures' fear grew keener. But not Witon's. He knew; knew it was naught but a blessing and with it came a surge of the greatest happiness he had ever known.

With adrenaline coursing fire through his veins, he shoved his arm upward as if to plunge the magnificent sword into the very sky itself.

They saw it then; they understood, and their fear vanished. Now, the booming cheers shook the earth with their ebullience. Hands were raised in worship to the sky and the Stars, to the dais and the rulers.

Amidst the thunderous ovation, Witon brought the blade back down before his gaze.

"What is the name of this great blade?" he asked Swerin, as he studied the shaft intently.

Engraved on the enormous blade were seven lines of text and, though each line used a different language—for some a different alphabet—Witon knew that they all proclaimed the same message, *the* message: *The peaceful co-existence of the Species shall reign forever.*

"It has no name, Sire," Swerin said, still with creator's pride bright upon his chubby cheeks. "It is for the owner to name it, not the creator."

Witon nodded; the Dwarf was correct. But Witon knew also that this great sword would serve as more than a weapon, and it would not always belong to him, but to whomever sat upon the throne of Witonia. He would give it the name it deserved.

Raising it once more in the air, where sparks of the sun's golden light bounced off it and on to the smiling faces all around him, he named the blade.

"Good Creatures, I give you… The Sword of Swerin!"

Once more, the cheering reached a fever pitch and though Swerin tried to argue, none would hear it, even if they could. With a deep bow, he returned to his own throne.

Witon knew the time had come to address the Creatures of this realm, and he went to take a seat upon the throne, planning that from here, he would make his Coronation speech. But, as he looked at the faces and the magical quilt of existence they created, he knew he could not. He looked around him to the Council of Creatures. Witon offered them a humble shrug of his shoulders and turned back to the assemblage.

With a purposeful gesture, he removed his cloak and his jewel-encrusted crown and laid them reverently on his throne. He walked forward to the very edge of the dais and sat down, hanging his long legs over the edge, his hands folded meekly in his lap. With silver eyes afire, he scanned the crowd. The expectant silence thickened, filling the mammoth space, the very air, with terse anticipation.

"Today, you make me your King," Witon began and his small smile spoke of his own bewilderment. "I may, in fact, be your king, but in truth, I am but one of you. I am the same as any Dwarf who wishes to create things of magic and beauty, not tools of war. I am the same as any Centaur who wishes nothing more than to live among the trees without fear of an arrow. I am the same as any Faerie who has no wish to be someone's pet. I am the same as all of you—one who believes in peace and freedom and a life where anything, any dream, is possible if you truly believe.

"I do not, I will not, rule this nation, but I will care for it under your rule. You will decide," Witon pointed a firm finger at the entire assemblage, "through the Council of Creatures, every law and statute this country will follow. Ye will not answer to me. Nay, I, and all my blood to come, will answer to you."

Witon stared at the Creatures of this new world, connecting his gaze with as many as possible, hoping they saw in his face his truth and sincerity. He stood up and reached a hand back in Belamay's direction. The Queen rose, came to his side and took that hand. He turned to the Council behind him and motioned for them to step forward, to stand beside him. They formed a line on each side of him, the most dedicated, determined, and devoted creatures he'd ever known, and his heart swelled to bursting.

Witon turned to the hundreds of smiling, tear-stained faces, faces of every shape and color.

"Go now and celebrate. Eat, drink, and make merry. Celebrate not for me, but for us all—all of us who have come to live in freedom… in the great Kingdom of Witonia."

THE END OF THE BEGINNING

Dear reader,

We hope you enjoyed reading *Birth*. Please take a moment to leave a review, even if it's a short one. Your opinion is important to us.

Discover more books by Donna Russo Morin at https://www.nextchapter.pub/authors/author-donna-russo-morin

Want to know when one of our books is free or discounted? Join the newsletter at http://eepurl.com/bqqB3H

Best regards,
Donna Russo Morin and the Next Chapter Team

About the Author

Donna Russo Morin is an award-winning historical fiction author. Donna has dabbled as a model and actor, working on Showtime's Brotherhood and Martin Scorsese's The Departed. Branching out with her storytelling skills, Donna is now a screenwriter. A graduate of the University of Rhode Island, Donna lives on the south shore of Rhode Island close to the ocean she loves so very much. She is the proud mother of two sons, Devon and Dylan, her greatest works in progress.

Visit her website at
www.donnarussomorin.com
Friend her at
http://www.facebook.com/
Donna.Russo.Morin
and follow her at @DonnaRussoMorin.

Books by the Author

Birth (Once, Upon A New Time Book One)
The Courtier of Versailles
Gilded Summers
The Flames of Florence (Da Vinci's Disciples Book Three)
The Competition (Da Vinci's Disciples Book Two)
Portrait of a Conspiracy (Da Vinci's Disciples Book One)
The King's Agent
To Serve a King
The Secret of the Glass

Lightning Source UK Ltd.
Milton Keynes UK
UKHW041827160421
382135UK00001B/90